Melville

by
Greg McBride

AmErica House
Baltimore

First printing

ISBN: 1-58851-534-6
PUBLISHED BY AMERICA HOUSE BOOK PUBLISHERS
www.publishamerica.com
Baltimore

Printed in the United States of America

*Dedicated to all men who love women
and all women who doubt men's motives,
which should cover just about everybody.*

Chapter 25

Jake Stark eased along the wall of the falling down tenement building, shadows of the night concealing his every movement. He felt the rough bricks cutting into his back as he slid along, but ignored the pain to concentrate on the task at hand. His progress slowed as he approached the corner of the building, firelight and shadow pushing at each other as the bonfire in the center of the square before him danced in the night. A quick look around the edge showed him what had to be done. Several raucous, drunken thugs surrounded the bound and gagged woman that Jake had come around the globe to save.

The daughter of the most influential man in Israeli government, her father had the cash and the pull to get the best when Muhjahadeen radicals had snatched her from her car at a stoplight. The best was Jake Stark, known in his profession as "The Axeman."

As Jake steeled himself to leap out and eradicate his few remaining enemies (the four sentries already having been taken care of), he stopped and said into thin air, "I've got an artistic dilemma here."

"What are you talking about, artistic dilemma?" I asked as I stretched my aching shoulders. Here I am, on the last chapter, and Mr. Muscle-bound decides to get picky.

"Even I can't take out 'several' guys at once. How many are in a several anyway? Is that like a gaggle?"

"All right smart guy." I edited and punched in "four" instead of several and wrote in a group of gas barrels on the far side of our imperiled, and of course, beautiful heroine.

Jake paused and said, "That's better, at least I can work with this."

The Axeman lunged catlike from his cover; the worn, but cared for, Smith and Wesson 4506 leaping into his adrenaline-dampened palm. His first Teflon coated, 250-grain slug penetrated to the center of the piled fuel barrels, erupting into a blazing fireball that destroyed two of his opponents before they knew he was there. The third man didn't have time to secure his weapon as Jake's Smith roared and bucked twice in quick succession. The "double tap" caught the armed terrorist square in the chest, the second slug slightly higher than the first, just like his firearms instructor had taught him so many years ago.

Jake swiveled his waist to gain a target acquisition on the last man and saw, too late, the blossom of flame erupting from the barrel of his opponents Chinese made SKS.

Stark felt the 7.62x39 slug impact his left shoulder even as he raised the Smith in his right hand and executed another flawless double tap.

He felt no satisfaction as he watched the last man fall to the ground, simply the cold emptiness that has forever been the way of the warrior. Chances were good, he thought, with a sardonic smile, that he would fill that emptiness the same way it had been done for thousands of years.

He walked over to the prone girl and removed her bonds, helping her to her feet. She threw her arms around his muscular neck and asked in broken English how she could ever repay him. Jake looked down into her beautiful upturned face, lit by the fires all around them, and the answering fires held in her eyes. As the sound of the rescue chopper assaulted their ears, he leaned closer to her, his hard lips bare inches from her soft, yielding mouth and said, "Do you have plans for dinner tonight?"

THE END
Look for number # 51 in the Axeman series, coming soon.

Chapter 1

That last part I typed in just because if I didn't, my editor would, and I was tired of giving him the pleasure of doing anything to my manuscripts. I downloaded the whole thing onto an empty 3.5 diskette and slipped the loaded disk into an envelope. An envelope that I took from the stack behind my battered IBM word processor that sat on my battered desktop, in my battered den, in the center of my battered life. The old lady at the post office called these submissions "little pieces of my soul," and I'm not so sure that she isn't right.

I tried to straighten my back and got only the satisfaction of pain lancing through my shoulders and neck. I squinted at the antique clock on the wall beside me (antique simply on the merits of its age, and plus the lady at the garage sale told me it was), and doing some quick math in my much befuddled mind, decided that I'd been at this for about twelve hours. Long enough to earn one hell of a stiff neck.

"Come on," a voice said, very close to me. "I just took a slug with no complaints and you're letting a little bout of stiffness worry you?"

I squinted my tired eyes at the figure I could just make out leaning against the doorframe of my den. As my vision adjusted for anything beyond twelve inches in front of my nose, a hardened mercenary came into focus. Six foot five inches and two hundred and fifty pounds of muscled violence potential, with jet black hair and an unruly forelock reminiscent of a more famous hero. His face had a classic, and very cliched, chiseled look. His eyes were the only original feature he possessed, non-descript, plain, brown eyes. His eyes were mine.

"Dammit Jake, you told me you'd leave me alone for a while after I finished this one." I reminded him peevishly. I'm not so far gone that I don't realize there's something really wrong with reminding a figment of your imagination of a promise he made you, but I just couldn't help it.

"So you could do what? Sit around on your dead ass and do nothing all day long?" The big, burly man stepped closer to me, settling one hip on the edge of my desk.

"Maybe, but I deserve some kind of reward. Twelve hours is a new record." I started out good; "I might just look into that vacation I've always wanted to take. Now that I've got some money in the bank, it might not hurt to spend a little of it."

"Oh yeah, right." Jake's confidence in me was staggering. "You're not going anywhere, why don't you just face it?"

"I'm outta here." I shook my head at "My Personal Hero" as I pushed past him, out into the living room of my little one bedroom house. Being mad as hell, and not watching where I was going, the first step I took, I felt something under my foot and heard a small squeak. I lifted my bare toes carefully and peeked down through tightly shut eyelids, afraid of what I might find.

Breathing a heavy sigh of relief, I bent down and picked up the small gray bundle that was chittering at me for almost squashing his tail. The chinchilla crawled quickly up my arm and took his favorite perch on my shoulder with no small authority, letting his bushy tail wrap around the back of my neck. Just like he owned the place.

"I thought I told you to get rid of that rat," Jake's perturbed voice cut in.

"You'll go first, Deltoid Boy," I answered him. I don't know why Jake would be jealous of the fuzzy little guy, but then again there really is no way to guess what your average hallucination is capable of. I guess as such things go, Jake really isn't too bad to have around. When he came to me and set me to putting down the adventures of his life, I had been unemployed for six months (damn that Sears and

Roebuck for closing their catalog business) and was quickly running out of options. When the first of the Axeman books had sold for an amazing amount of cash, I moved Jake and I to this tiny town in northern Montana in order to get away from it all. And having never been at the center of it all, I assumed that this was it. The town of Browning only had about twelve hundred people in it, but it was just a short drive to the metropolis of Great Falls, which boasted an international airport (meaning that they had a Latino janitor) and all of the important things in life. Mainly, they had a McDonald's. My main reason for bringing myself here was for the view. The entrance to a national park is just up the road apiece, and the mountains are so close, you feel like you can reach out and touch them. Yeah, it's a cliché, but if you could look out my living room window every night like I do, you'd say the same thing. I found a little house just outside of town that had been empty since the old man who'd built it had died a few years before. It didn't take me long to get settled in and start writing, and that had been almost three years and fifty books ago.

Jake and I? Oh, we got along pretty well, which is important if you're going to continue to imagine someone. Our snappy repartee was constantly flowing until the moment, well, until the moment I tried to talk to someone else, then I might as well forget it. My brain locks up the store and goes out to lunch for the rest of the day. I usually end up feeling really stupid and wind up spending the rest of the day doing affirmations (me and Stuart Smalley).

I walked through the living room with fresh and tearing eyes, the bright sunlight of early spring in Montana, and my enforced twelve-hour den sabbatical made everything seem a little newer. I looked closer at the used bargain basement furniture, including the garage sale end tables and shaking my aching head, decided that maybe newer wasn't the right word. Maybe just a little different. At least I tried to stay towards one color. Earth tones. Whoopee.

I grabbed my keys off the kitchen counter on my way through the house, the fuzzy pellet maker chirping in my ears as I passed by an old butter dish full of raisins on my "antique" kitchen table (yep, same little old lady that sold me the clock). Fishing out a couple for each of us, we left the house, and hopefully Stark behind.

The chinch happily devoured one of his dried up grapes as I stood staring at my aging Ford pickup. The poor old truck was slowly settling to its hubcaps (the two that were there, anyway) in the gravel of my driveway. I wondered how much longer it would live before giving up and in a flash of concern for its health, decided that the chinch and I would walk to town. It was only about a half mile down the winding dirt lane that was Mamut Road (so named for the old man who had built this house and talked the county into building him the aforementioned road). Besides, it was spring and there would be plenty of wildlife for the rodent on my shoulder to look at. It was good to get out like this, to try and get back to nature in my own weak little way.

The gravel crunched beneath my feet as I walked down the winding road away from my obsessions and towards what passed for civilization in "these parts." I cursed beneath my breath (not being the type who usually curses above his breath) as I felt a minuscule piece of gravel work its way into my left Payless Special through a worn spot in the sole and come to rest in the most painful spot possible. By the time I reached the Pet Store on Main Street, I was limping like I'd lost a leg in the war.

The Chinchilla was chirping with delight as I pushed open the door and was hit by the usual pet store smells. Yep, you guessed it, fish water, bird cages and cat litter. When we were through the door the fuzzy little rat on my shoulder let out a kind of a high pitched squeal, which was answered immediately by the woman that popped up from behind the counter.

"Hey there, Melville," she spoke to me as she held out her hands to the fuzzball. He covered the four feet between us in one leap, landing in her arms. She cuddled and cooed at him for a minute before looking back up at me.

"You name him yet?"

"He hasn't told me what name he likes yet." I answered her as best I could.

"Well, he will," she said launching into a one-sided discussion about chinchillas in general and this one in particular, which she'd had for two months before I'd bought him from her a few weeks ago. The owner of this pet emporium is a married woman of somewhere around thirty-five (I'm smart enough not to ask). Susan Oaks stands about five feet tall and would probably weigh less than one hundred pounds soaking wet. She's got kind of blonde hair and blue eyes that just never seem to miss anything. Susan and her husband Eric really do make a pretty good couple. He's about six feet or so with dark hair and eyes and is as laid back as a man can be, a natural defense mechanism for life with his better half. Between the two of them, they make up about one hundred percent of the people in town that will put up with my social inabilities. One thing about Susan though, is that she really gets a kick out of her job. This town has less than its share of stray animals thanks to her finding them all homes or keeping them in her store window until she managed to shame someone into taking them. She actually made me fill out a psyche test before she would let me take the chinchilla home. Sue said it was to make sure I would take good care of the little pellet maker, but I still wonder...

The long aforementioned conversation was slightly one-sided because my attention was now riveted on the roll of duct tape that Susan had apparently been using to fix a broken glass counter top. Now the tape was just lying on the counter, making my foot throb. I didn't interrupt Susan's diatribe for permission; I just grabbed up the tape, sat down in one of her straight-backed chairs and went to work. I removed the offensive piece of gravel from my shoe, and seeing no wastebasket, carefully stuck it in my shirt pocket. Replacing my abused tennis shoe, I did two quick wraps with the duct tape and tore it off with my teeth. Standing up to test my repairs, I sat the duct tape back in the exact same spot it had been the moment before. Walking up and down the aisle of couple of times, I noticed, too late, that Susan's monologue had come to a sudden halt sometime during my ministrations.

She was just standing there, hands on hips, staring at me with a kind of blank look on her face.

"Sorry," I stammered, "I didn't think you'd mind about the tape..." my defense petered out, as she walked right up to me, reached inside my shirt pocket (a little personal I thought, even if we were pretty good friends), fished out that one piece of gravel, and looking at me the whole time, dropped it on the floor of her pet shop. She continued then, lecturing me on the evils of improper care of rodents, as though nothing had happened.

As the chinch and I exited stage right, aka Snagglepuss, two hours later, I was happy to have given Sue someone to talk to other than the animals. Besides, let's face the facts here, I really didn't have an over-abundance of friends, and Susan and I got along really well. I got along great with her husband too, and that kept me out of a lot of trouble. The people in town had even gotten to the point where they didn't spread rumors about us anymore. Eric and Susan were both good people to be around, putting up my social faux paux as if nothing were wrong.

Walking down the main street of this quiet little town towards my original destination of the tiny post office, complete with its one-hundred year old postal matron, I saw two girls of about ten coming down the sidewalk towards me. They would have passed without incident if the chinch hadn't decided to scold them from his partly hidden vantage point inside the collar of my shirt. Both girls screamed in terror at the sight of the fuzzy rat and then laughed, pointing at me and whispering to each other.

Oh God, I thought, they probably call me that weird old guy that lives at the end of Mamut Road. Which is only about one step above being Mr. Withers, that weird old guy who runs the amusement park. Right, Raggy? I ducked my head and walked a little faster towards the end of the block. I burst through the door of the only federal building in this town and was not surprised to find myself alone with the blue-hair behind the counter.

"Well, hello there, Melville." She squinted at me through her bifocals. "Sending another piece of your soul off to New York?" (I told you.) She laughed at me (well, cackled) as I smiled back at her.

"Yeah, I guess so." I handed over my latest labor of love, with enough cash for the government to take it to New York for me and said good-bye. As I walked out the double doors, back out into the world, I heard the old crone's voice calling to me.

"See you in a couple of weeks!" Most likely.

Crap. A tall, dark-haired man was leaning against a light post waiting for me to leave the relative safety of the post office. I quickly walked past him, my head down, not even wanting to acknowledge his existence. Looking up half a block later, I was not surprised to see that he had fallen into step beside me. A very active figment of my imagination and "my personal hero," Jake simply looked at me with that smug expression of his as we walked down Main Street.

"Where are we going?" he asked.

"I'm going to see that travel agent Sue told me about." I answered, tight-lipped, glancing around quickly to see if anyone was watching that crazy writer talk to himself again.

"You don't want to do that." Maybe it's not what Jake said exactly, but that was the general drift of what he said all the way down Main Street and through the front door of the old gas station that had been recently converted into the Midland Travel Agency.

A new business in a town of this size usually caused quite a stir but Susan had told me that the single young woman who owned Midland really fit right in with the other relaxed business people in the Chamber of Commerce. I suddenly realized that Sue had used the word "single" at least five times in the course of our conversation. According to my pal the matchmaker, the woman waiting on the other side of this door was just my type. It was actually a relief to me that Susan knew what my type was, having no idea at all myself.

Finally, as I stood in the lobby letting my freshly repaired tennis shoes sink into the brand new carpeting, I could take no more of Jake's endless commentary. "Oh, would you just shut up!" I even said it louder than I meant to. I closed my eyes, praying silently that no one had heard me.

That hope evaporated into thin air as I heard someone clear their throat. Someone distinctly feminine. I opened my eyes slowly and turned to see a young woman looking at me with that "who the hell is this crazy man in my building" expression on her face. But, bless her heart, all she said was "Are you...all right?

Her voice had that certain huskiness that Kathleen Turner held pencil erasers behind her teeth to accomplish. She was dressed in a simple white silk shirt and blue jeans with light brown hair that reached to her shoulders. Not tall, not short, her figure was what I would have to call perfect, and as I met her gray eyes with mine, her delicate perfume hit me right in the pit of my stomach. You know how really good perfume does. It just snakes in through your nose, down your throat, grabs your stomach and gives it a good, hard twist.

One delicate eyebrow arched up to disappear under her bangs as I watched absolutely fascinated. Fascinated by the flair of her nostrils as she breathed, the way she crossed her arms across her chest, the way she looked like she was considering calling the local mental institution to see if anybody had escaped. Every bit of her enraptured me.

"She asked you a question, dillrod." Jake's voice again in my ear.

I snapped my dangling jaw shut with an audible click and stammered an answer in what I hoped was a positive manner. Well, I was as all right as I was ever going to be.

"In that case," she said, "how can I help you?"

She approached within three feet of me, my mind telling me that I could feel her body heat on my face. Boy, did it feel nice.

"Uh," my mind froze, locked up tighter than Al Gore's sense of humor.

"Uh," I repeated the word, trying to jump-start my lingual abilities, when the wave hit. A drowning, crashing wave of self-consciousness swamped me as I stood in the middle of the travel agency lobby, staring at the Playmate of the Millennium. Was my fly open, my shirt wrinkled that crusty stuff in the corner of my eyes? Her body's heat on my face became the burn of an honest to God blush.

The chinchilla took the opportunity presented by the lull in the conversation to come around to my shoulder and chitter happily at the woman who would be my travel agent for the rest of my life.

Her response to the little rodent was instantaneous.

An unbelievable smile lit her features, and she dropped about ten years from her already youthful appearance. Her eyes fixed on my cuddly little shoulder warmer, and she took another step closer to me. To us. To him! Glancing at me quickly for permission, she reached to pluck him carefully off my shoulder, cooing at him while she held the chinch against her chest. I'd swear that little rat was giving me a look that said, "I'm where you want to be, and I know it."

Envious of a furry little rat. I realized then, in a blinding flash of insight, that I had to get a life. The Goddess walked back into her office, clucking over the little bastard like a mother hen. I followed her with no little trepidation, trying to keep in her mind that the object of her present affection and I were inextricably linked.

"So," she said, not looking up from her bundle, "what can I do for you?" She sat behind a cluttered "office depot" desk, waving me to one of the chairs in front of her. I took a quick look around the office and was shocked to see a very familiar looking "antique" clock hanging on the wall. I didn't know that garage sale woman had more than one clock. I was entertaining a mental image of some old lady sitting on an assembly line turning out hundreds of those clocks when The Goddess asked me if I would take a seat. Please.

Okay. I sat down, forcing myself to look relaxed. Crossing my legs, I started to say that I really just wanted to get away for a while when I noticed that The Goddess seemed to be staring at something. My shoe. When I looked myself, I saw the dull gray gleam of duct tape. With my old friend self-consciousness foremost in my mind again, I whipped the offending Payless Special back below the desk, out of her sight.

"Where?" she said, looking at me with those destructively intelligent eyes. It took a few seconds for what she said to sink in, and I heard Jake again, "Talk back to her, dummy."

"Where what?"

Jake groaned as the lady gave me another one of those "crazy man" looks.

"Oh!" the word fell out of my mouth followed by others that

were far less meaningful, if that's possible. "I don't know, I guess just anywhere."

"Okay," T.G. said as she rose from her seat to reach the pamphlet rack behind her. I was mentally composing a thank you note to Rocky Mountain Jeans when she turned back around and handed me a bunch of brochures.

"Why don't you take a look at these and get back to me." She released the chinch, which bounded across the table, climbing my left arm to his shoulder perch.

"Okay. Great. Thank you." I got up and walked quickly out of the office. My main thought was to get the hell out of there before I made an even bigger ass out of myself. By getting to the street without having to say another word, I figured I had a better chance of ever being able to face this lady again. I stopped outside her door and realized that she hadn't told me her name. There on the carefully lettered front window, under the legend Midland Travel was the name Mary Byrd. I said the name quietly a couple of times until my own reflection came into focus on the glass. I stared at myself in silence for a moment before I realized it was I. Baggy jeans that were torn and faded enough to be in fashion six or seven years ago. A worn flannel shirt suited for early spring in the mountains, but not the cover of GQ. All topped off by a face I've always thought of as integrity laden, the aforementioned non-descript brown eyes and long, dark, stringy hair barely held in check by an old Tigers ball cap.

Oh yeah. Nothing like a first impression.

"Okay, okay...." it was Jake again, "so you're no fashion plate, maybe she's not into materialism."

I looked at him with a puzzled expression. "Thanks for the help, Jake, but even if she's not into materialism, that still doesn't mean she's into slobs." I was more than a little bit worried about Jake's sudden bout with being supportive.

"True enough." Even Jake now sounded depressed.

It made me feel better that at least he wasn't being kind to me out of some sense of pity.

"Oh yeah," he said, "it is pity, but you only deserve so much."

Knowing Jake like I had for three years, he had always kind of acted as my own personal anti-confidence. No matter what I was doing, my buddy Jake was there to tell me that I was screwing it up. Today wasn't the first time that someone had caught me talking to myself. I would always swear that Jake waited until he was sure I would be caught before making an especially rancid comment, and there I'd be, waving at the air and telling a figment of my imagination to shut the hell up. I don't understand why I can't have a normal imaginary friend like everybody else, you know, one that talks to you when nobody else will and doesn't take your favorite Weebels (not to mention the Weeble play palace) and hide them. Well, the good thing is that I haven't been committed yet, and M.P.H. (My Personal Hero, pay attention please) has come close to making me a millionaire.

Chapter 2

We were on the road home before either of us spoke again.

"What am I gonna do?" I asked no one in particular but just like always, Jake answered me.

"You've got it that bad for her, huh?" At least he was grinning at me when he said it.

"I've got it way worse than that, buddy. I never really believed in love at first sight before, and then, 'BAM' right between the eyes like a Louisville Slugger in the hands of the Babe himself. She just makes me feel all..."

"Warm and fuzzy?" he asked.

"Yeah, that's pretty much it."

"What do you think it is?" Jake asked.

"About her?" I asked. "I don't know. Her hair, her eyes, her smile. Just everything about her I guess." Looking down at my shabby appearance, I waded on. "She's like some magical Snow White, and here I am, dumpy, frumpy, unkempt, wrinkled and at least three other evil little dwarves that I can't remember."

"Maybe Mopey, Sleepy, and Doc?" Jake was trying to be helpful again.

"Thanks, buddy," I said, still eyeing Jake nervously, "but what chance has a loser like Yours Truly got with a smart, pretty, successful woman like that?"

"Hey now, Mel," Jake rallied to my defense, "don't go countin' yourself out of the race before it even starts. Have you taken a look at the balance of your checking account lately? The town bank is probably gonna name the new wing after you. Just because you don't like to act like you've got money is no reason to forget about it."

"What good is it though if I'm overdrawn in the personality department. All the money in the world can't buy you true love, I'm proof of that." Don't you just hate those old clichés, especially when they apply to you? "If all your money can't get you what you want in life, at least it can get you in the ballpark." Jake was trying to be cryptic.

"Meaning..." I hate cryptic people.

"You've got a lot of choices that you can make here, things that you can do with that cash that you couldn't do otherwise. You can buy yourself some decent clothes if you want. Hell, you could get enough plastic surgery done to make yourself into, well, whatever you want to look like."

At the mention of surgery, I was more worried than ever about M.P.H.'s sudden turn towards benevolent patronage.

He must have read the look on my face because his next words were, "Hey, do you think I've lost count of how many women you've given me in the last fifty books? Sixty-seven. All of them young and beautiful, so if you want this gal, then I'll do anything I can to see you get what you really deserve."

"You think we've got a chance?" I asked him with little confidence.

"Absolutely," came the answer from my imaginary friend.

"How did we manage 1.3 women per book?" I asked.

"We managed them very well, thank you." Jake's answer was ever confident.

"Look at you." Jake was back to his same old wonderfully endearing self by six a.m. the next morning, driving me out of my nice, warm bed with his annoying, and true, opinions.

"What?" I mumbled at him.

"You've spent so much time in this house that you can hardly put one foot in front of the other without falling down."

"... walked to town yesterday." My mouth was not really responding to my brain's commands yet. I thought my past efforts should amount to something, but I had forgotten the important fact that I was dealing with a crazed mercenary.

"Not even close. Get up, you're going for a run."

"Go to hell." I rolled over, pulling the covers back over my head in an attempt to shut Jake up. He was silent for a moment, planning an attack I figured. I was right.

"Do you remember the way her perfume smelled?"

"Damn you, Jake." I decided to go for a run.

It was almost seven-thirty before I got back to the house and I was ready to kill Jake no matter what it took. Electric shock treatment, a Prosaic the size of a tennis ball, whatever. There was no way that my poor aching body was ever designed for this kind of abuse. I still am a firm believer in the fact that if God had intended us to run everywhere, he would not have let Henry Ford get past the first grade. Please remember that Forrest Gump only had an I.Q. of seventy, otherwise he would have taken the bus everywhere he went instead of running. Did anybody else ever wonder why he never wore out that one pair of shoes?

By the time mid-morning rolled around, it found me again in my dark dungeon of a den, sitting there staring at my abused IBM, wondering where the next Axeman best-seller was going to come from. "What are you doing?" Jake asked.

"I was gonna start on the next book..."

"No way. We've got a woman to woo." I'll tell you right now that there's nothing quite like hearing a hardened mercenary use the word "woo."

"What do you know about wooing women?" I wanted to know, not to mention the fact that I just love using that word.

"Actually, I know everything you know, it's just a matter of using what we have..."

M.P.H. and I stared at each other for a minute, both of us looking worried.

"Or maybe knowing where to look?" I added to Jake's statement carefully.

"Yeah," we both said much relieved.

The magazines hit the table with a resounding smack, causing everyone in the small public library to turn and give me a shared scowl, and bless their little ol' hearts, one big Shhh.

Oh great, I thought, "weird guy" looks from half the town now. I've been getting way too many of those lately. I sat down in one of the creaky, old wooden chairs, afraid this would invoke another round of 'shushing' from the gathered escapees from the Shady Pines Retirement Home, but apparently it was O.K. to make noise with a chair because their collected wrath didn't fall on me again that day.

"That's the price of leading a public life instead of being a nice, comfortable hermit, Mel."

Jake's hand hit my shoulder as he leaned in to see what I was reading. "What have you got there?"

I just gave him the same look the Geritol Club had just used on me. He knew I couldn't talk to him in a place like this, but like some kind of psychotic older brother, he just kept trying to get me in trouble.

I opened the newest issue of *Cosmo* and looked at the table of contents.

"What Women Want In Men." Jake was reading over my shoulder, "Sounds promising. Hopefully, there's an article like that in every one of these rags."

Whipping my pocket notebook out of, well, my pocket, I dove headfirst into the world of the "nineties" woman.

In three day's time, my notebook was full and I was totally confused, and the library staff was convinced that I had no life whatsoever. Bits and pieces from all of those magazines led me to a really fuzzy idea. Women seem to want men to be able to read their minds, to do the right thing without being told. They want to be treated well by the men they're with and by the other men in their life. Isn't that pretty much normal though? Doesn't everyone, male or female, just want to be understood by the people around them? Pretty good insight for a sequestered author, huh? You try spending your glory days with a typewriter on steroids and an imaginary friend and see if your mind doesn't wander a bit.

Being in here for the last three days solid pouring over every back issue they had of women's magazines, I'm sure the librarian thinks I'm studying to be gay or something, but she's old and doesn't talk to anyone much anyway. Anyway, it would seem that women just want what everyone wants. Now, if I just knew what that was.

In the meantime, the running never seemed to stop. It just went on and on. The country out here is beautiful, but let's get real here, you don't give a damn what the mountains look like when you're trying to spit up a lung. Jake never let me give up either. I think it's kind of like having Tony Little for a workout coach. (Is there a more annoying person than that?) He kept me running almost every morning with threats and promises of what it would be like if I didn't, mostly threats like, "Oh yeah, she's the kind to go for a deep, loving, sensitive, only slightly pudgy writer." That one almost always worked. Endless sets of push-ups and sit-ups became an everyday part of the new me, and in very short order, I started to feel a lot better. I wasn't tripping over everything anymore; my body was doing what I told it to, not whatever it wanted. More importantly, I was beginning to gain confidence in myself, something I'd been without for a long time. It was a slow start, but it was something.

Not to mention the fact that every time I got near that word processor, Jake would not let me sit down and write. He said it was a kind of training thing that I needed to be completely attuned to the task at hand if we were going to pull this thing off. And I really think that he was right. Most people go through their whole lives and never pull off the one big thing that would make them better than the average person. They just go on losing all the magic in their lives a little bit at a time instead of using it all up in one giant flash. It's kind of a theory of mine that everybody is born with just so many positive things that can happen, and if you just stumble along without really caring, it'll get all used up with the day to day things. You know, like when the traffic light changes just as you get there so you don't even have to take your foot off the gas, or when your groceries add up to an exact amount in the express lane.

I didn't want to use up my magic like that, I wanted to blow it all at once, and that's what I was going to do. I was going to get this lady or die trying. Besides that, I get most of my life's theories from late-night TV, so it's no big loss if it doesn't work out.

Chapter 3

"Okay." M.P.H.'s voice cut into my personal hell, "Clothes are next."

"Huh?" I looked up from my last pushup in a set of (gee, millions?) to see Jake's reaction to my very complicated question.

"I said 'clothes,' Mel, you need new clothes."

"You know," I rolled over and lay in a puddle of my own rapidly cooling sweat, "I don't even need to argue with you there." As I stared at the spackled ceiling, my time in front of Mary's office desk came back to me in a rush. Duct tape. "Shoes?" I wanted to know, "Can we get shoes?"

"We can get all the shoes you want, Mel," Jake grinned at me as he dropped a towel on my face, "just as long as you remember your checkbook."

The little bell on the pet shop door did its little ding-a-ling thing as the new and improved (at least on the inside of my ragged out clothes) me stepped through it into the crush of small animal noises.

"Hey, Melville." Sue spoke from the back store room, "Whatya doin' today?"

I dumped the chinchilla on the counter where he immediately began to dig into trouble.

"Not much." I answered her, "Um...are you doing anything this afternoon?"

"Well," she came out to face me, a devilish look in her eyes, "what'd ya have in mind, big boy?" She smiled at me in the way she knew damn good and well would make me blush. I suddenly became very interested in the floor at my feet as I felt a rush of heat on my cheeks.

"No, really," I stammered, "I need a favor..."

Near hysterical laughter was her only answer and my blush deepened as I picked up her line of thought, right down in the gutter.

"Oh, come on..." my laughter joined hers until the chinchilla distracted us by tipping over a peanut jar full of pens.

"Okay, okay, okay." Susan wiped her eyes with the back of her hand and looked at me as we gathered up the give away pens from all over the counter. "What do you need?"

"Well, I need some help with my wardrobe and I was thinking of going into the big city today."

"And you want me to go with you?" She looked interested at least.

"I thought you might get a kick out of helping me spend my money."

Sue got a kind of thoughtful look on her face as she said, "You know, somehow, I never think of you as having a lot of money."

I let her think a minute before I asked, "What do you say?"

"I say let me call Eric and lock the doors."

We were on our way.

A trip into the city was always an adventure in the "MelMobile," the old Ford truck coughing and wheezing its way down the road as if every second would be its last. I was fearless though, possessing that special kind of naiveté that comes from having never been left on the side of the road by a broken down vehicle.

Susan, on the other hand, apparently knew what walking was like, and I was getting a kick out of watching her wince in fear each time the pick-up let out a particularly bad cough. I didn't have the upper hand for long though.

"So," she asked with an innocent expression on her face, "who's this all about?"

I'm almost sure that my jaw unhinged for it to be able to drop as far as it did. I was beginning to wonder if Sue might actually be psychic as I gained control of the situation again for a split second by bobbling the steering wheel so badly that we almost ran into an overpass. But the fear passed from her eyes as she repeated the question, like there was any doubt that I had heard it the first time.

"What do you mean?" I almost stuttered as I asked, completely blowing the "smooth" approach my panicked mind was trying to work out.

"You know what I mean, Mel." The look she gave me was sharp, a warning not to insult her intelligence in a blind rush to discredit what she'd said. "Who's the girl?"

Something about the look in her eye told me that she already knew the answer to her question, but I also knew that she wasn't going to let me off the hook that easy.

No reason I couldn't give it a try though. "You know who she is."

A slow smile came to her face as she answered, "I know, but I want to hear you say her name. I want to hear it come out of your mouth."

I frowned at her, hoping to make her think that I wasn't going to give her the satisfaction. Finally though, my eyes kind of fogged over with an involuntary memory of her as I said the name, "Mary Byrd." In a few seconds I snapped back to the present and turned to Sue. "There, you happy now?"

Sue just kept smiling and said, "Found out what I wanted to know." She was still smiling when I exited the interstate and headed for downtown.

As the two of us stood in front of the most exclusive men's store in the city (which meant that they didn't sell hardware as a sideline). I found myself wondering why I was forcing myself to do this. All the things about how she should love me as I am were running through my mind at a breakneck speed. In a heartbeat I realized that any woman who'd take me as I am wasn't worth having.

I think that while I was having life revelations, the only thought on Sue's mind was to see how much of my money she could spend.

I would swear that she actually licked her chops before grabbing my arm and towing me through those big glass doors.

Immediately we were set upon by an irate salesman with an overweight, retired cop of a security guard shifting from foot to foot (aka Barney Fife) behind him.

"I believe you have the wrong establishment." The first words out of his mouth were enough to send Mama Melville's favorite son scurrying for cover, which I would've gladly done if Sue had let go of my damn arm. As it was, I was trapped like a deer in the headlights.

Susan looked this stuffy, confrontational head salesman in the eyes, directly through his seven hundred-dollar eyeglass frames, and told him, "Nope, we've got the right place. But you've got the wrong attitude."

Ooh, Susan—1, stuffy guy—0.

Taking a quick stock of my appearance, I couldn't help thinking that this salesman should want to sell us some clothes, but it was obvious that he was confused about his current location. Obviously, this scarecrow of a man thought that he was on Rodeo Drive in Beverly Hills instead of downtown Great Falls, Montana. The salesman (who was wearing a really nice suit, I also noticed) took a deep breath to order the guard to throw them out, but before he could, Sue was at him again.

"Do you work on commission in this establishment?" the last two words were a mockery of the tone he had used moments before.

"Why, yes of course..." he answered, off his guard. Sue wasn't going to let him up now that she had him on the ropes.

"Who's the worst salesperson you have? Or which one do you treat the worst?" Susan was really on a roll, and I was just wishing that I had the slightest idea where she was headed.

He stuttered for a moment and pointed to a mousy teenage girl that was polishing the gigantic windows with a wad of soggy paper towels, "That would have to be Tina, we don't even allow her near our regular clientele..."

"Good," Sue ran right over him and the security guard with me still flapping in her wake like a paper doll. "She'll do perfectly."

I would like to think that we did our best to change Tina's life that day. I did hear that she told that scarecrow where he could put her job before the day was over (didn't sound anatomically possible to me), and I also saw a few years later where she had graduated from design school and started her own firm in Great Falls, but that is another story...

I had taken Susan along for a good reason, knowing that by myself, I would only buy one cheap suit and run for home. Having a whole new wardrobe in mind, Sue was here to spend some serious coinage. Suit after suit was brought out and tried on for fit until one was found that met with both Sue's and Tina's approval. Now the real fun would begin. I was afraid. Very afraid, and I had good reason to be.

Fabrics of every type and color were felt and compared, chosen and rejected. I quickly lost count of how many different suits I tried on in that cramped little dressing room. No one suit we bought was like any of the others when all was said and done. For the first time in my life, I was beginning to feel like a real clotheshorse, instead of the poster child for the Scrawny Lumberjack's Association.

Without me noticing it, they moved on to casual clothes sometime in mid-afternoon. Slacks, sweaters and loafers in endless variety and quantity.

My head was cocked off to one side, with a mix of horror and disbelief on my face as I looked into a three-way mirror that was edged with overweight little cherubs. I was dressed in tan slacks and a knit polo shirt with an off white sweater thrown across my shoulders. Yuck.

"This isn't even funny, Sue..." was all I needed to say.

"You're absolutely right, Mel, no way the sweaters will work." Susan was draped across a chair that might have been Louis, as if I knew anything about furniture. "You look like a yuppie from the boring part of Hell."

"What makes you say that, Buffy?"

"Ooh, a rapist wit to boot." Sue laughed.

"Don't spread rumors about me, Sue, the word you're looking

for is 'rapier.'"

"Tina," Susan called the flushing salesgirl over to them, "we've got to think stylish here. But with Mel, good style isn't as important as any style at all, after so long without...style." Susan even looked confused for a second; "Do you see what I mean?"

"Thanks a lot, Sue."

The cascade turned to T-shirts with bright prints and a hundred different variations of blue jeans. Casual shirts of every kind were given the nod time after time, all colors, and all styles. I even managed to score a pair of Doc Martins. Pretty cool, huh?

Finally it was over. The sun had gone down hours before and we had purchased every decent piece of clothing in the place. As the two of us approached the counter to settle the bill, the snooty head salesman appeared out of thin air at the smell of money. The clothes were being loaded into the back of the pickup by the hastily recruited cleaning staff, and it was time to start Tina's college fund.

"Are you ready, sir?" Our friend the head salesman still looked doubtful.

"Yeah," I answered, "I think we're done."

"Which gold card will you be using then?"

"Gold card?" I'm sure that I looked a little confused.

"Yes sir, your credit card?" the salesman began to smile his evil little smile as the smell of blood joined the scent of money on the air.

"Credit card?" The look on my face had not changed, and to Susan's obvious horror, was not showing signs of changing any time soon.

Sue grabbed me by my "I'll wear my old clothes out" flannel shirt and drug me to the side.

"You don't have a credit card?" she was almost in a panic.

"No," my face still mirrored confusion, "why? Do I really need one?"

Susan's voice rose an octave as she asked, "How do you plan to pay for all this?"

A slow, even smile spread itself over my face as I answered Sue. "Wanna watch?"

Perplexed could not even begin to describe the state of Susan's mind as she followed me back to the polished glass counter, and the aforementioned clerk.

"How much is it?" I asked as I approached the register.

The salesman's smile deepened as he stated the numbers. That smile dropped down to his shoelaces as I pulled a roll of bills out of my pocket and counted off a good share of them. Sue's jaw dropped too when she saw the denomination of the bills was "Thousand."

I spoke as I finished counting out twelve bills, "The extra goes directly to Tina, and you, sir," I stopped and looked at the shocked salesman, "close your mouth, would you. You've got a little bit of drool running down your chin."

I really thought Sue was going to pass out. She didn't stop laughing long enough to eat her fries until the bright lights of the city were miles behind us.

"I'm really sorry, Susan. I'll pay you back for dinner as soon as we get home..."

This threw her into another fit of laughter. The look on the face of the poor girl working the drive-thru when I had tried to pay for two fries and two shakes with a thousand dollar bill was apparently more than Sue could stand. She waved a hand at me as she caught her breath again.

"Don't worry, Mel, I know where you live."

Chapter 4

"Wake up, Lazy..." There was no compassion in Jake's voice at 6:00 a.m.

"C'mon Jake," I started to plead, pushing my face deeper into my pillow; it was a late night.

"Tough, you still have to get up and get moving, and while you're doing that, I'll come up with a plan of attack." Jake sounded determined.

I rolled out of bed and stood there in pain as my brain sloshed back and forth in my skull. "She's a girl, Jake." I spoke when my head stopped making those sloshing noises. "Not a drug dealer's jungle palace."

"Only difference is the weaponry, Son." M.P.H.'s smile was more than a little bit smug and I was starting to get the first of many bad feelings.

When I had drug myself back from yet another run to Hell and back, Jake was waiting for me with a smile on his face, and the beginnings of a plan. (One of these days I'm going to ask him why he never goes with me when I run.) I drug myself through the shower as Jake continued to talk. It was starting to seem like I drag myself everywhere these days.

"Okay, what exactly did we learn in three days with *The Ladies Home Journal* at the library?" Jake asked as he draped himself across my worn out couch.

I was still adjusting my jeans and T-shirt, and checking myself in the mirror when Jake's question caught me a little by surprise. I hadn't thought about my research project for several days and I had to grab my notes off my desk to refresh my ailing memory.

"A woman's self confidence can be bolstered without being obvious. She must feel good about herself to care about someone else," I started.

"Or else you can get an emotional cripple that depends on you for everything," Jake interjected.

Looking at Jake with no little surprise in my eyes, I said, "Very good, Jake, and that goes for both men and women." Again, I'm not so far gone that I can't see the humor in discussing psychiatry with a figment of your own imagination, but at this point, there's not much I can do about it.

"Men or women, absolutely." Jake agreed with me, and waved his hand for me to continue.

"Her clothes should make her feel good..."

"I don't think we really care about clothes here, Mel." Jake interrupted me, sounding a little bit annoyed.

"I think we do, Jake." I tried to explain what I'd discovered in the library, plus the fact that I'd spent a whole day reading about women and their clothes, and I wasn't about to waste all that information. "I think you can tell a lot about how a woman is feeling, in part at least, by the clothes she is wearing." I continued reading from my notebook, "...make her feel good with blues and greens denoting tranquility, reds and yellows describing sexiness or turmoil, and white being the color of innocence."

"Innocence?" Jake was incredulous now.

"Yeah, you know. Didn't you ever feel like the world was brand new?" Me, a writer, struggling to convey a thought.

"You mean like at the beginning of a book?" Jake's thought came in a flash.

"Right, just a little bit naive. But you always lose that by the end of the second chapter."

"Okay, I understand what you're saying. What else did you find out?" Jake asked.

"She is more likely to accept compliments if the source is considered non-threatening, and she should be constantly reassured of her beauty and her life."

"Very high maintenance." Jake looked kind of annoyed again.

"Maybe so, but I think we'll both agree that they are definitely worth it." I leaned back in my chair, lacing my fingers behind my head and smiling as Mary's face came to mind.

"Oh, c'mon, Mel, there's got to be more than that..." Jake said.

"Well actually, that's pretty close to it. The rest of the stuff I kind of already knew. Like the way she has a hundred little signs to let you know what she wants you to do next. You need to be able to tell what she's thinking by staying attuned to her every little move. All people have a basic need to be understood without having to tell the other person what they're thinking." I stopped, a little surprised by my speech.

The look on Jake's face gave way to shock as he said, "You're pretty good at this."

I smiled and said, "Remember, interpretation and expression of ideas is how I make my living, M.P.H." I rubbed my hand on my fifty dollar pair of jeans and added, "And I make a pretty good living."

My Personal Hero apparently thought I was getting too cocky for my own good as he asked, "Then why haven't you had a girlfriend before? If you're such an expert at all this?"

My tipped back chair came to the floor with a crash as I started to think, searching for the answer to Jake's question.

"First off, my friend, I never claimed to be an expert at anything. I probably know less about women than any other man in the entire world does. As far as why? You know, I think I bought into that "it will happen to you when you least expect it, it will happen to you someday." That kind of crap. Now I realize that it won't happen until you make it happen. If you sit on your butt waiting for happiness to come to you, all you get is calluses. I don't think I ever really tried before, or I couldn't try for some reason."

"Not a real mystery if you think about it for a second, Mel." Jake said, again hitting the proverbial nail on the head. "It's just your complete lack of self-confidence."

I absorbed that carefully, "I think you're right, Jake. But we've set out to change all that."

"Aw, c'mon Susan," I was pleading now because I was getting nowhere, fast. "You've got to help me out here."

"No. No way am I gonna do this to another woman, it goes against our silent code."

"Code?" Was I on the verge of a gigantic breakthrough in the field of relationships? Something no man had ever found out before and lived to tell the tale? Could this be the one thing that would get me the woman of my dreams?

"Yes, code," she continued, "you know, never go to the bathroom alone, always enlighten the man in your life by taking him shopping, and never, ever throw another of your own sex to the wolves."

So much for that big secret, but the rest of her statement brought me to a halt for just a second before I leaned over the counter with what I imagined as a dangerous smile on my face. "You really think I'm that dangerous? Really?" It almost made me feel like I was at least in the running.

Sue looked at me long and hard, "Two months ago, I would've said no, but now I'm not so sure."

The bell above the pet shop door chimed as I turned to look for an ally in my argument with Susan. Eric stopped in his tracks when he realized something was up.

"What?" The poor guy was almost shell shocked, as Sue and I just stared at him.

"Eric," I started in on him before he even had a chance to put his lunch box down, "you've got to help me out here."

"Sure, buddy," the tall man said, eyeing his wife over my shoulder for silent cues, "what can I do for you?"

"Help me convince your wife to have a dinner party." The answer to my problem was simple, at least to me.

"What for?" Eric was not willing to jeopardize his fine standing with his better half without a clear idea of what was going on.

"So we can send the sheep to slaughter," Sue said angrily.

"Oh," Eric's surprise hid a sudden smile, "you mean the charming Ms. Byrd?"

"Yes," I was going full steam now, "Mary. I need a plausible reason to run into her again and a dinner party at your house would be the perfect setting. You know, no pressure, just good friends sitting around talking about anything that comes to mind. I need a chance to show her that I'm something more than the stammering idiot that wandered into her office without any idea where he wanted to go on vacation."

Eric looked over my shoulder at his wife and said, "You're right, he does have it bad."

"Argh!" I screamed at the pet store ceiling as I stormed out the door.

Another argument came to me in a flash as I stood just outside the door, and I was ready to burst back in when I heard Eric say, "Why do you do that to him? You've been planning that dinner party for weeks, Mary's already been invited, hasn't she?"

I was sure Sue was smiling as she said, "Of course she has, but I wouldn't want any man to think he's in charge, now would I?"

Standing in front of my mirror (I've been doing too much of that lately, I know) I started to wonder if I'd overdone it with this suit. The cut of the jacket kind of made me look like a gangster, but maybe that's not a bad thing. I still remembered Sue's comment about any style being better than none at all.

"All right, Franky," I snarled my best Bogart at my reflection, "you crossed that invisible line, you broke the unwritten rule, and now you have to pay."

"John Wayne?" Jake's voice came from behind me.

"If it's that bad, I don't think I'll try it at the party," I smiled at my reflection, my confidence at an all-time high. It's a wonder what a new suit can do for a man's soul.

Jake straightened my tie for me as he said, "You just relax and leave the attitude up to me tonight, this poor girl will never know what hit her."

I showed up at the Oaks' house early with the idea of helping Susan get dinner ready but was promptly run right out of the kitchen. I found Eric in the living room and received an appreciative whistle for my "civilized raiments."

"Okay, huh?" I asked as I turned around to show off my newly acquired "wise guy" image.

Eric looked down at his own jeans and casual shirt. "Well, if you take off the jacket you'll make me look better."

"Okay..." I hoped I sounded as doubtful as I felt, "but I don't have shoulder pads in my shirt."

Eric chuckled as he asked, "And where did you get the matching suspenders and tie?"

I held up my brightly patterned tie for inspection and said, "All you have to do is call up the 'Larry King Live' show and ask for the order line..."

"Now remember," Jake whispered in my ear as I heard a car door slam in the driveway, "smooth, cool, confident. She'll tell us what to say. You just let me tell you what she wants to hear and she'll melt like butter."

When the doorbell rang I yelled to Sue in the kitchen that I would get it. I stopped for a second in front of the door to gather my new cache of confidence around me like a burial shroud and whipped open the door, thoroughly scaring the unsuspecting woman waiting on the other side.

"Oh, sorry..." were the first words out of my mouth and the night was off to a fine start.

Susan came out of the kitchen to do a minimal introduction, and to make an attempt at saving my life. "Mary, I think you already met Melville once."

The Goddess looked at me with a charming, blank look on her face, visibly racking her brain for what in the hell Sue was talking about. She apparently came up empty because her next words were, "No, I don't think so, Sue."

"I..." stammering to answer before Sue could, I saw recognition in her eyes before I finished my statement, "I was in your office a few months ago, looking to take a vacation."

There was no way for her to hide the shock that came into her eyes, there was just too much of it. "Oh yes," she answered, "I didn't recognize you without a chinchilla on your shoulder."

Sue laughed and took Mary by the arm, leading her into the kitchen. She threw a look over her shoulder that told me to go back to the living room where I belonged. I swam through the haze induced by the lovely Ms. Byrd's perfume and found Eric still on the couch, blissfully immersed in his own ignorance, drinking his requisite Heineken.

It took a little doing, but eventually Susan filled me in on their conversation in the kitchen, and it went something like this.

Sue went back to stirring a cream sauce as Mary tested the glass of white wine she'd just poured herself. She wondered if alcohol would be the only way to get through this night.

"Sue," Mel's goddess spoke slowly, "what have you done to me?"

The innocent look on her hostess' face was pushing into the realm of comical. "What do you mean, Mary?"

"Setting me up with Melville in there," a casual wave of Mary's left hand covered the little writer in the living room. "You didn't warn me about that."

Sue's face turned serious, an unusual expression for her. "Okay, I won't try and tell you that I don't have hopes for you two, but I know there's no quicker way to doom a romance than to set two strangers up with each other."

Pausing just long enough for Mary to get in an obligatory nod, Sue waded right back into the one-sided conversation.

"So you can see that this is not a setup. Truthfully, you've been in town for a few months now and you don't seem to have any close friends here," she paused again, "do you?"

Mary shrugged her shoulders. "I just don't make friends very well."

Sue pointed to herself, "Neither do Eric and I, and neither does Mel. I'm guessing you had plenty of invitations, but you just didn't feel like you fit in with them. I'm right, aren't I?" she added as Mary's expression turned just a little bit indignant.

Mary just stared at her friend, not the first person stunned by Susan's remarkable insight. That dubious honor belonged to her husband Eric. The whole story, including a '65 Cadillac, a bottle of cheap champagne and their wedding night, will remain untold because of a death threat. A serious death threat.

"I took a chance and invited you here tonight because I thought you might just fit in with this bunch of miscreants. Okay?"

"Okay." Mary was still a little stunned.

I lowered myself into the couch with my patented "out to lunch" look on my face. Eric just watched in wonder as the minutes passed and my expression didn't change. Finally, I spoke. "Isn't she beautiful?"

"Well..." Eric started, "I guess. If you like that sort of woman."

I turned to face my host with a little attitude. "Sort?" I wanted to know. "Sort! How can you refer to the mother of my future children as a sort!"

Eric laughed as I sat back in the couch with a smile on my face. It was the smile of a man who knows what he wants and has it within his grasp. "I just hate men that are too pushy." Mary was on her second glass of wine and was starting to feel like a lush. But Sue was being so good about keeping up with her that she decided to continue.

"I know it." Her hostess waved an agreeing (and slightly intoxicated) hand around her head. "They think they know everything."

"It just really bothers me when they try and tell you what you want." Mary was feeling very adamant.

"Absolutely." Sue was still agreeable. Of course at this point, she would have been agreeable to almost anything.

"Or how about when they think they can tell you how to fix all your problems in about ten seconds. Real, live, dyed in the wool fix-it men. Don't they realize that when you tell them your problems, you just want someone to listen to you for a second or two? Is that so hard to figure out?"

"That's what's great about Mel," Sue inserted his name into the conversation with a sly glance at her guest, "he doesn't try to force anything on you. He's just really relaxed, a good friend."

Mary favored Susan with a threatening look. "Careful, careful." She wagged a finger at the cook in a mock warning.

Although the actual dinner itself had been delayed forty-five minutes due to the amount of alcohol consumed by the hostess and the guest of honor, the table had been set to perfection, the crystal and silver gleaming in the light of the Sears and Roebuck chandelier that had been in Susan's family since it was purchased in 1935. Grandma Guinness would be very proud.

I straightened my tie for the four thousandth time in the last hour and rocked my head from side to side as I took my eleventh hour instructions from a figment of my own imagination.

"Remember, Mel," Jake whispered from my shoulder, "smooth, cool, confident. I'll tell you what she wants to hear."

"Right," I was trying to convince myself, "this is going to work."

Reading my doubt, Jake said, "I'm just another part of your own mind, Mel."

"So, if you screw this up," I interrupted him, "it's still my fault." Jake patted my shoulder, "Pretty much."

"Great."

I know Eric was watching me as I struggled to maintain the illusion that I still had some control over my own life at this point. And I think that he was almost feeling sorry for me until I really started to screw things up.

As we all sat down to eat (well, pick at) the lavish meal Sue had prepared for our benefit, I valiantly attempted to engage Mary in conversation with a well planned and thought out question about the travel business.

"How's business?"

The Goddess was taken slightly aback by the suddenness of the question but she was willing to make an effort too.

"Good."

Snores were heard at Susan's end of the table, followed by a solid thump as her head hit the surface.

Everyone laughed, as Sue loudly demanded that a more engaging conversation begin immediately. I smiled across the table at the charming Ms. Byrd, and was thrilled when she actually smiled back. Jake started whispering advice into my ear, and I asked, "Okay, Mary, how is your new business going really?"

Still a little flushed with laughter (and wine), Mary told me that things were going as well as she had expected. New businesses were always slow at first and she was sure things would pick up when summer started.

Jake was again whispering in my ear as I said, "Well, I'm sure you're right but, if you'd do some little things, I'm sure that your business would pick up right away."

Mary looked at me then, with a quizzical look on her face. "What do you mean?"

"She's listening to you," Jake whispered, "all women want is for someone to solve their problems, and now is a good chance to show her that you know a little something about business. Show her how intelligent you really are."

"You could run specials to different destinations, make a greater use of advertising, or several other things. A business like yours has a lot of potential if you just work at it a little."

She batted her eyelashes at me. "Do you really think so?"

I really thought she was serious at this point, so I decided to help her out as much as I could. "Oh yeah, you could really have quite a business on your hands with just a few ideas. For instance..."

"Mel!" Sue was really being loud, interrupting me just when things were going my way. "No more business. Talk about something else, anything else."

I smiled my most confident smile (looking back, is confidence just another form of ignorance?) and asked Mary where she was living.

She smiled at me again (this stuff really works) as she said, "I've got a little house rented over on Pine street. It's not much, but it's all right for now, until I find a house I want to buy."

"You don't want her to buy a house, dummy," Jake was feeding me my dialogue again, "you want her to live with you! You'd better take care of this right now. You're an intelligent man, think of something. Maybe she doesn't know much about real estate..."

"Buying a house right now would be a mistake anyway," I said with a casual wave of my hand, my battered psyche spinning its wheels in vain to substantiate what I'd just allowed to leave my mouth.

I got blank stares from all around the table for a couple of seconds before Mary asked the obvious question. "What makes you say that?"

My mind was still running through the gears to come up with a way to cover my own ass. Funny thing about this situation, I hate people who talk about something they know nothing about. I guess that should've given me my first, and most important clue.

"Well," I said as slowly as I could, trying to give my line of B.S. more strength, "the market around here has really fallen off in the last six months, I wouldn't want you to get taken or anything."

"If the market is low, isn't that a good time to buy?" She was batting her eyelashes at me again. "I don't know much about these things, you know, being a woman and all." Mary was twisting a lock of her hair around her index finger and warning bells were starting to go off in my head.

"You might think so." I took each step carefully, expecting the ice to cave in underneath me at any moment. "But actually, a low market means that all the good houses have been taken, and you just need to wait for a good one to come back on the market." Jake was screaming for me to change the subject, and I agreed with him.

Taking a long deep breath, I said, "Have you ever tried deep sea fishing?"

Chapter 5

Sue told me later that she managed to catch up to my Goddess just outside the front door. Mary had simply shaken her head at my last question, mumbled something about "bullshit" and walked out. "Mary..." Sue pulled on Mary's arm to stop her, "I am so sorry about this..."

Ms. Byrd turned to her distraught hostess, "Oh come on, Sue, I know that. Give me some credit, would you?" She stopped here with a puzzled look on her face. "The funny thing is, I know that whoever that was in there, he isn't the same guy who was in my office. That guy was cute in a dumpy, frumpy sort of way. This guy is some kind of used car salesman from Hell." She shuddered involuntarily. "He's just plain creepy!"

"I know, I know," Sue agreed, "there is no way that Mel could've been any less himself tonight. I don't understand what happened, but I'm sorry to have put you through this."

Mary looked at Susan for a moment with her arms across her chest and a scowl on her face. Slowly though she started to smile. "All right, I'll forgive you this time. But I gotta go."

She turned to walk away as Sue added, "Thanks for coming..."

A derisive snort was Mary's only answer.

I was listening in the living room when Eric blocked her way as Susan came back into the house. I'm sure killing one mousy writer was foremost on her mind. Susan stopped when she bumped up against her husband's chest. Favoring him with one of her "withering" looks, she barked, "What?"

"First off," Eric began, "those looks have never worked on me, never will. Second, we've got to have a talk about Mel before you go in there."

"Talk about what? How I'm going to kill him?"

"Something's wrong with Mel." The tone of his voice stopped her in her tracks.

"What do you mean?" Susan was concerned now.

Eric shook his head from side to side. "I don't know for sure what it is, just that something's not right with our young friend. So I don't want you to be too hard on him, Okay?"

What her husband was saying finally got through to her and Sue looked worried as she asked, "Do you think we can help him?"

"I think we can try, but I'm afraid that it's something he needs to work out for himself."

I just sat on Eric's couch with my head in my hands, knowing that Sue would be in to kill me very, very soon, and knowing that I desperately deserved it. Jake wasn't chattering in my ear anymore, and I found myself praying, for the first time in a long time, that he'd never come back.

I just couldn't believe what I'd done. I'd embarrassed my friends and myself and most important of all, Mary thinks that I'm the kind of guy that I hate with a passion. I couldn't even begin to think of a way to change the way she was going to hate me after tonight. I wasn't even sure if I should. Maybe I didn't deserve a woman like her, maybe all my instincts were right. No man who would pull something like I tried tonight deserved to live, let alone in the company of such a lady.

A long, slow groan escaped my lips as I sagged back into the couch. Susan was standing in the living room doorway looking at me in pretty much the same way she'd looked at me when she took that piece of gravel out of my pocket. It was the kind of look you give something you don't really understand, but you are kind of fascinated by the question of what might happen next. Somehow, I didn't think this was going to be so simple.

She just stood there, looking at me for what felt like hours before I finally broke.

"I don't know, Sue. I just don't know what happened."

Susan looked at me for a moment more before she spoke. "I think you do."

By the next morning, "my personal hero" was back in my life as much as ever. The tall, bulging mercenary sat down on one arm of the earth tone (a classy way to say brown) couch that I'd paid fifteen dollars for at yet another garage sale, and watched me finish out my last set of pushups.

Jake had a very apologetic look on his face as I stood up to go take a shower. It would be my second already today, but the early summer day was hot and muggy enough to drive me into a cold shower. The other benefits of such bathing practices were obvious. Not to mention necessary.

"Mel, I'm really..." he started to apologize before a word from me cut him off.

"No," I barked as I started to walk away from one very dejected fiction hero figment of my imagination. "No way, Jake, just leave me alone."

As usual, Jake didn't listen to me at all, following close behind me as I entered the kitchen. "Really, Mel, I'm awfully sorry, I had no idea that she would react to us that way. I thought we'd studied all the angles and had it all figured out."

"Jake." I was exasperated with M.P.H., but my anger was losing steam fast. "I'm not sure that this is the way to do it with this lady. I think it would be the smartest if I would just be myself with her."

Jake just looked at me for a second before he said, "You don't believe that, do you?"

He wasn't trying to run me down; he was just speaking the truth. I just couldn't see how a woman like (sigh) her would want anything to do with a guy like me. She was stylish and sophisticated, at least when compared to me. And I was, well, just myself.

"Bastard." I cursed at M.P.H. and myself as I walked into the bathroom.

When I emerged from my shock shower, my mindset had improved dramatically and I felt better than I had in hours. I was feeling almost hopeful as I walked into the living room and plopped down in my worn out easy chair, the footrest popping up of its own volition. My mind was spinning with ideas to win back the favor of The Goddess, none of which had a snowball's chance in hell. I knew that I needed a gigantic flash of inspiration, a sign from God above or at least...a decent idea.

Apparently, Jake could tell that this was the time to try to slip back into my good graces.

"This was definitely not the approach to use on Mary," he started off by stating the obvious, "what we need is a new plan."

"Right." I was in deep thought now, ignoring the fact that Jake was really trying. "We tried the women's magazines with no luck at all. I mean, we learned a lot, but it wasn't anything that we can apply to The Goddess. What else is specifically geared towards women?"

"How about romance novels?" Jake asked.

I shook my head at him. "I'm not that desperate, yet."

We sat in silence for a few seconds before, at the same instant, we both snapped our fingers and said, "Talk shows!"

With a raft of blank VCR tapes and a quick swipe to get the dust off of my little used Zenith TV, I sat down to glean what I hoped would be infinite knowledge from the likes of Oprah, Sally Jessy, Maury, and Phil. Looking back, I should've known better.

This took longer than I expected. After nearly one hundred hours of mind-numbing TV viewing, a common thread slowly began to form. In among the endless stream of men who used to be women and the men who loved them, and the lesbian clown accountants who date police officers, came a few solid thoughts on the part of these gurus of talk.

Oprah (men who breathe, how dare they?) had a guy on her show that had written a book about how if a woman puts you into the category of friend, they will almost never let you be more. I wasn't sure if the poor guy was going to make it out of the studio alive or not, and having experienced that particular phenomenon before in my short, and wildly unsuccessful love life, I felt a little sorry for the guy, when it became obvious that the women in the audience were never going to admit to anything like that. Ms. Winfrey had the audience ready to tar and feather someone for the first time in years. She stated on a national television show that women just need someone who cared about them as a human being.

This idea baffled me for the longest time, having no idea myself, of how else to treat a woman. I figured that must have been part of my problem, being sick that day in sixth grade when they pulled all the guys aside and taught them how to treat a woman like dirt, and make them like it. Hey, I always figured that if you're gonna cut class, pick the right one. Ah well...

Next came Sally Jessy (love me, love my glasses) with the grand idea that a woman's love for someone who is her lover and her best friend cannot be surpassed, except maybe by Sally's own love of tearful reunion shows (haven't we all had about enough of that?). I've always wondered about the "best friend" thing, you know what I mean, starting with a platonic relationship and working your way up. Sounds like a great idea if it can be pulled off. Again the idea of a woman permanently placing a man on the disabled list once she had decided that he was a friend came to light, and again it met with something other than acceptance. I think it was the same poor guy from the Oprah Winfrey show, he must have been making the talk show rounds.

Phil and Maury pretty much came up with one idea between them, Marla and Connie apparently having much the same personalities. They seemed to believe that a woman just wants someone that's comfortable to be with (which I find kind of convenient for them). A person they would want to build a life with, someone that will be there when she needs him, the guy that will treat them well and always be romantic, that kind of stuff.

I taped over one hundred hours of talk show drivel to glean these tiny nuggets of information. They have to be very important; at least I hope they are. Hinging the most important thing in my life, my non-existent relationship with T.G., on the combined knowledge of the oracles of afternoon talk, I decided to go for it. Platonic friendship that is.

Chapter 6

It had been almost a month since the dinner party when I again found myself on the doorstep of the Midland Travel Agency. It was now mid-summer in the mountains, only days until the Fourth of July. The heat was stifling, and the air conditioner above Mary's door rumbled to me as I stood outside in the harsh sunlight, hoping that things wouldn't be too cold on the inside.

My reflection in the plate glass window told me that I was dressed more appropriately than I had been the last time. Just decent jeans and a dress shirt, but a giant improvement over the starving writer attire I'd been wearing before.

"All ready to go kiss up?" Jake asked from behind me, opposed as he was to apologizing for past behavior, no matter how terrible it had been.

"Yep," I answered him with no visible dismay, using a small amount of the self-confidence I had built up over the last month of preparation for this moment. I didn't want to use up too much of the carefully guarded stuff and get stuck in the "uh" mode again. "And you keep your mouth shut the entire time I'm in there." I wasn't asking him, I was telling him. I've found that you have to stay in control when you're dealing with these imaginary heroes or they just run all over you, and we can't have that.

Pushing open the door and finding myself once more on the still fresh carpeting brought back a rush of self-doubt that I barely managed to battle back with my poor, wounded psyche.

The chinchilla chirped on my shoulder as he recognized the scent of someone, he hoped, would make a fuss over him. Recognizing that the same scent had a completely different effect on me, I looked at the chinch out of the corner of my eye for a moment. I was mentally chastising myself for pulling a cheap trick like bringing the rat with me, but I needed something to get me through the door. Figuratively speaking of course, I thought as I wistfully looked over my shoulder at the door and the safety of the street beyond.

Mary came bustling out of her office with a smile on her face, a smile that I saw fade when she realized that it was one of her least favorite people in the world who had darkened her door. Thanks a lot for your help, Jake, I thought, thanks a lot.

I felt the temperature in the room drop about ten degrees just like I had expected it would as she asked, "What can I do for you?"

God, I love this woman, was the only thought on my mind at the moment. Even when she's mad as hell, she's gorgeous. I told you I had it bad.

I threw both hands out in front of me, palms out in an ancient gesture of appeal (I had a vision of the first cave-dude trying to pick up a woman with the same gesture. Of course, he had a club stuck down the back of his loin cloth and as soon as the unsuspecting woman came into range, expecting a gift in the form of flowers or a dead mammal of some kind, it was "whack!" and back to the cave, Baby. Is that the way it all started? Anyway, back to the story...) as I said, "I came to apologize for the dinner party, do you think you can even hear me out?"

She took a half step backwards with a look of shock on her face as I thanked the gods of inspiration (or was it desperation) for the effects of brutal honesty. The Rat, bless his little heart, chose this particularly tense moment to run to the floor and chitter at Mary to pick him up when he reached her feet. She did so, holding the chinch close to her heart. He gave me that "I hope you're jealous" look, but this time I just smiled at him, and promised that I would remind myself later to feed the little guy raisins until he was ready to explode.

The Goddess gave me one of those long, slow, pursed lipped

looks and said, "Okay, come on in."

As she sat down behind her desk she looked at the fuzzy pellet maker for a moment before she spoke. "That was a really dirty trick to use him like that."

I hung my head low and told her, "I know it, but I didn't think I had a choice."

"Maybe you didn't," she answered with some fire still in her eyes. "Has he told you what name he wants yet?"

I laughed as I sat back in my chair. "You've been talking to Susan, and no, he hasn't yet, but he will."

"Maybe he doesn't want to tell you." She held the fuzzy rodent up next to her ear for a moment, listening intently.

"Well?" I asked.

Mary shook her head, "Nothing yet, but Sue said it might take a while." T.G. actually smiled at me as she said, "I like Sue and Eric, they're good people."

I nodded in agreement as I gathered my courage around the butterflies in my stomach that had been brought back by her killer perfume.

"I really can't tell you how sorry I am about the way I acted at that party."

Again brutal honesty did its work as she looked at me with her eyes wide open and said, "Try."

Maybe I was starting to warm to my task a little, but it still took everything I had to look her in the eyes as I said, "I'm really sorry." My sincerity was honest as I continued, trying to explain something that I didn't really understand myself. "I can't even tell you why I acted the way I did, but I will tell you that it'll never happen again."

I let her think about that for a moment before I played my hole card and said, "I think you know I don't usually act that way."

It was risky, but it paid off this time. Mary smiled again as she said, "Look who else has been talking to Susan."

"All I want from you," I said, "is a chance to make it up to you. Over lunch." I looked at the clock on her desk that read 12:01.

She laughed at that, almost causing my heart to explode, and said, "Oh, you're good all right." Then I saw a cloud come over her face and knowing what caused it, I made one more desperate move.

"But I don't want you to think that this would be a date or anything. Just a lunch, as friends." The cloud I had seen instantly lifted from her features, but she needed a little something extra to push her over the edge. Inspiration struck again. "I'll even let you feed the chinch."

Mary laughed aloud this time, her head thrown back in a strange kind of graceful abandon (and don't think that I wouldn't be seeing that image for the next couple of days). "Okay, you're on."

"Over lunch," I'd said. At least my faculties had chosen to stay with me in that particularly stressful moment. Now I wasn't sure it was such a good idea. We sat facing each other over a couple of club sandwiches and a piece of lettuce for the chinch. I was using every piece of witty banter in my scanty repartee and having light to moderate luck as my lunch companion fed the squirming bunch of gray fur on her lap. It was really pretty scary but I managed to sit back with some degree of detachment and watch my harmless charm and utterly non-threatening persona begin to break down her barriers of mistrust and privacy. She soon began to open up to me, slowly at first, but gaining speed, until she was telling me about her first date when she was a gawky freshman in high school. That was when I began to realize for the first time that we were truly perfect for each other.

We parted company in good spirits; her smile gave me some feeling of hope, and her promise to not be so hard to convince about lunch next time making me feel good about what I'd done. Until I remembered that it amounted to a bald-faced lie to pretend a harmless friendship with this lady when my ultimate goal was so much more.

Like I'd said before, this was a very familiar position for me to be in. Ever since, in the midst of a bout of teen angst, my dear mother had comforted me with the fact that all worthwhile loves had their start in friendship. Needless to say, I soon discovered (like that poor guy trying to sell his book on the talk shows) that once a woman has slid you into the category of "friend," it takes an act of Congress (or

God) to get you back into the active file. I'd had more than one of these absolutely heart-breaking relationships, and while they hurt like hell, they didn't turn my stomach like telling Mary what to do with her life (well, trying to tell her what to do).

This was also the point in my life when I realized that it was not a good idea to ask your mother about matters of the heart. It must have to do with their skewed opinions of the children they've given birth to. Whatever the reason, it's just not a good idea.

So why did I think it would work this time? I guess that maybe it was just that I believed, in my heart, that Mary was different than the other girls I'd traveled this road with. I didn't have a choice, at this point, to believe anything else. My heart wouldn't let me.

Busting through the front door of the Pet Store screaming, "It worked! It worked!" really wasn't such a good idea looking back on it now. But in my own defense, how was I supposed to know that Sue had picked this afternoon to let all the birds out of their assorted cages for a mass cleaning? By the time the dust (and feathers) settled down, we had most of Susan's highly agitated inventory back in their cages.

The sawed off business owner was picking the last brightly colored feather from her hair before she finally asked, "What worked that's got you so excited?"

"Mary and I, that's what." I smiled like I'd swallowed one of the canaries instead of stuffing it back into its prison.

"You mean that you and her..." Sue gave me a locker room grin and planted an elbow in my ribs. I'm betting that she had a lot of brothers. Older brothers.

"No, no. Not that." I back pedaled quickly, "She and I just had lunch though, and it looks like we're going to be good friends."

"Good friends?" She didn't look like she was happy for me. "You didn't buy into that old line of crap about women wanting both a friend and a lover did you?"

I'm sure I just stared at her for quite a while before I could say much of anything. When I could talk, it came out something like this. "You're telling me that the idea for the basis of my entire future is a line of crap? You don't have any idea..."

"What if she's right, Mel? What if it doesn't work?" Jake was back, helping out as best he could.

I sat down in a chair and buried my head in my hands, suddenly in the pit of despair.

"What if you are right, Sue? What am I gonna do?"

Quick as a flash, I jumped up, my confidence having caught up to me again, and it looked like it was going to stay a while this time. "No, you're wrong, Sue. She's different, I know it. This is going to work, it has to!"

I stormed out of the pet store much the same way I came in, leaving in my wake a very confused, and frightened, friend.

Chapter 7

Before long, it was almost a daily occurrence to have lunch with Mary. Sometimes Susan joined us, sometimes she didn't. I don't know for sure what she thought of how well Mary and I were getting along, for once she was keeping her mouth shut about the lives of those around her. I know that it wasn't easy for her, but to tell you the truth, it still made me nervous.

Don't get the idea that this time was easy on me either. Every single second that I was around The Goddess I just wanted to blurt out everything; how much I cared about her, how I would do anything for her, all the corny stuff you could think of. But I knew better.

M.P.H. was against me now more than ever, telling me at all hours of the day that this was by far the worst idea I'd ever had. Even threatening Jake with shock therapy had no effect on the muscled mercenary. Visions of him began to haunt my dreams again like they had when I was writing the Axeman series. He was always the bearer of the same message; get out now! He had no faith in Mary or me, and it scared me, that in the middle of the roller coaster of my emotions, Jake was still only a part of who I was.

Mary and I were getting to be very close. I realized this when she plopped down across from me at Mel's Diner one Saturday afternoon. The sunlight slanting through the window facing Main Street still bounced off her hair, making it shine even though it looked like she'd crawled out of bed and wound it into a ponytail. She wasn't wearing any make-up, again holding up my "just jumped out of bed" theory, but I didn't really mind because I'd always thought too much makeup was a really bad thing. My attractively dressed travel agent wore torn sweatpants, and a threadbare T-shirt. I laughed aloud when she leaned against the back of the booth and stretched her legs across to my bench. Her left Payless Special had duct tape wrapped around it. Duct tape! Mary looked across our booth at me with one darling eyebrow raised in a question. We weren't as different as I had thought. I stammered to answer her unspoken question, "I uh...you look kind of wiped out." She did look tired, but even that couldn't diminish her beauty one bit.

Mary smiled at me, suddenly full of life and happiness. "I am. Mel..." she paused for a second, a faraway look in her eyes and a goofy grin on her face.

"Uh oh," Jake said, "get ready to get kicked in the stomach..."

Mary continued, "I can't believe it happened to me."

"Here it comes." Jake again.

"What?" I nudged her arm gently, a smile frozen on my face, an empty feeling beginning to form in the pit of my stomach.

She took a deep breath and said through her wide smile, "I met someone last night..."

Mary continued to talk the usual stuff about how great this new guy was how well they'd hit it off, how they were going to see each other again tonight. I couldn't tell you for sure what she said exactly. My face had frozen the same inoffensive smile as always on my integrity-laden face, but behind that quiet mask, I spent a lifetime on the other side of Hell itself. Jake was utterly silent as I prayed to a less than sympathetic God to kill me now and get it over with. I found myself wondering why I'd willingly put myself in a position where I would be forced to sit here and listen to this one-sided conversation. I started to laugh quietly to myself, a silent, mirthless laugh that scared even me as I realized that I had done this on purpose, spent countless hours putting this woman at ease so she would feel she could tell me anything. Kind of like the anything she was telling me now.

Some far away part of my mind heard the rain begin to fall against the diner window, washing the summer dust to the street. It fell in huge, cold drops and I smiled again as I watched the people outside scurry for cover; my heart lightened a little to see other people suffering with me.

Eventually my eyes came back into focus as my mind came back to the here and now. Mary was saying something about how they had spent the whole night talking and he was just so great and handsome and all that other crap.

"Aren't you happy for me?" Mary's voice again broke through to me. She was looking at me, that killer smile not fading from her face, so sure of what my answer would be.

I swallowed hard and came up game. "Of course I am. I mean, I know how hard it is to meet that special someone..." I reached across the table to grasp her hand, and winced as I felt an electrical shock pass between us. Mary's smile faded as she looked at my hand and then into my eyes. Had she felt it too? Did she realize what it meant? Was this the moment I'd been praying for?

"Oh Mel," I saw the pity come into her eyes, and knew that she still had no idea of how I really felt about her. I was almost surprised to find that this was a relief to me. "I'm sure you'll meet someone very soon..."

The rain was falling harder than ever as I stepped out of the diner into the downpour forty-five minutes later. But to me, the conversation between Mary and I had gone no further than those words from her. A single tear coursed its way down my cheek, unseen in the cold rain that battered my face and threatened to chill my body to the bone. To myself, I quietly said, "I already found her."

Jake, to his credit, did not make an appearance to rub my face in my own stupidity for a couple of days. I had barricaded myself in the world of the Axeman and had written a complete book in a matter of forty-eight hours. I finally signed off on another version of the same old "hero gets the girl" story and looked up to find Jake beside me with a sympathetic look on his face. I reached for my wineglass, and upon finding it empty, reached for the wine bottle, and that was empty too. Having no choice but to face M.P.H., I turned to him and growled out the phrase, "What do you want?"

"Does it feel good?" he asked.

"What are you talking about, Stark?"

"Does it feel good to let the hero get the girl for a change," he answered.

"Damn rights it does," I yelled at him. "I deserve her, and this way, I'll make damn sure I get her." The alcohol was working, but it really hadn't changed my outlook on life.

Again, Jake was only a part of me, not letting me get away with anything. "You don't deserve her, Mel. You know she has to be won. You can never give up. If you want this friendship thing to work, you have to keep on being her friend, even when you don't want to 'cause things aren't going your way." His voice took on a nasal tone as he finished the sentence. The force of his statement stunned me to the core, but I still had to fight back.

"You were the one who hated this idea from the very beginning. You've wanted me to get out of this from the start, and all the sudden you get to act like you've been behind me all along?" I shook my head at him. "I'm not gonna let you get away with this, not this time!"

"You listen to me." Jake suddenly loomed over me as I realized that I was yelling at him. "I didn't want to back you in this until I was sure it was what you really wanted. This friendship ploy is probably the worst conceived plan since they designed the foundation of that tower in Pisa, but you're committed to it now, and I'm going to make you stick to it even if you don't want to."

"It's not going to work, Jake, you said so yourself." I wasn't yelling anymore, I didn't have the strength.

"And tell me," Jake said, "just when did you start listening to anything that I had to say?"

"But..." Now I was really confused.

"You can make this thing work, Mel. All you have to do is stick with it."

I sat for what felt like hours and thought about what Jake had said.

"You're right," I told M.P.H., "you're absolutely right."

"It's about time you realized it." Jake was relieved. "Now, go get cleaned up. Nobody buys the disturbed writer bit any more."

I looked down at down at myself and laughed. My first laugh in over two days. I was a real mess. The clothes I'd been wearing when I got home from the diner now reeked of my enforced sabbatical at my word processor. I looked in the hall mirror and laughed at my reflection. Bloodshot eyes, beard stubble and rumpled, oily hair. I was my old self again.

"Mel?" Jake was still in the den with my word processor.

"Yeah, Jake."

"This book you just wrote, that's you in there, not me. Jamison will never buy it."

"I know Jake. I know."

I never even made it as far as the shower before I heard an urgent knock on the door. I glanced around the house before answering. It wasn't too bad; having spent the last two days in the den lent to keeping the house clean. Throwing open my front door scared the hell out of both the women on my doorstep. Susan and Mary gave me the same look, one that clearly said "you dummy." Or worse. I realized that I should quit opening doors like that before somebody hurt me. Still a little shell shocked from my near emotional breakdown, and a little bit cocky from the wine, I leaned my head to one side and said, "Well, the two most gorgeous women in town on my doorstep and I'm fresh out of whipped cream." I stepped to one side of the door and motioned for them to come in with a grand sweep of my arm.

They walked into my living room with their eyes wide, and I realized that this was the first time either of them had been in my house. I found myself looking around too, and was not surprised to find the house as boring as it had ever been. "Would you two like some wine?" I asked, trying to be a good host.

Susan just gave me another funny look as she said, "Mel, it's only nine in the morning."

I gave Sue that same look right back as I said, "Really? Well, that's okay because I think I'm all out anyway." As they arranged themselves on my couch, I flopped down in my easy chair, the footrest instantly in position. Mary was staring at me with real concern in her eyes. Well, if not at me, at least staring at my condition. I looked at her for a moment, wondering how much she really cared, and why. I shook my head to clear the effects of the alcohol as I said, "I know I look like hell, but I just spent a couple of days at the word processor and I wasn't really expecting any company."

Mary's elbow caught Susan in the ribs, prompting her to say, "I wouldn't let Mary call, knowing how well you answer the phone."

Laughing, I said, "When I get going on an idea, I don't stop for much of anything. But don't think that you ladies aren't welcome here." As if to emphasize my point, the chinch did a half gainer off the curtain rod and landed in Mary's lap. Needless to say, she was thrilled even if she was just a little surprised.

After she'd calmed down a little, Mary spoke slowly as she said, "We were just worried about you, Mel. When you didn't show up for Sunday dinner yesterday, I didn't know what to think."

Again, I looked into her eyes for the answer I wanted to see. It wasn't there. I rose from my chair just wanting to get away from her before I said something we'd both regret, and said, "If you guys can hold on for just a second or two, I'll whip us up some coffee."

As I walked into the kitchen, I heard Susan say something to Mary about how she would talk to me. Sue followed me into the kitchen, waiting patiently while I started the coffee pot, then following me outside while I scattered cracked corn for the wild birds that frequented my back porch.

"Does she know?" I asked her.

She took a deep breath before she answered, "No, she doesn't."

"Good, that's the way it should be." I was relieved to know that I hadn't seen pity in Mary's eyes. That was the one thing that I wouldn't be able to handle right now, knowing that she pitied me because of how I felt about her.

"I don't know, Mel," Susan was worried now, "you haven't seen the way she's been acting. She really cares about you."

"The only trouble is, she doesn't know it yet." I finished for her.

I put my arm around her as we turned to walk back inside, and said, "Thanks for coming out, Sue."

She patted me on the back as she said, "One thing, Mel?"

I smiled and said, "Anything."

She wrinkled her nose at me. "Take a shower."

Two of my most favorite people in the world were sitting at my kitchen table drinking coffee, and talking to each other when I emerged from yet another in a long series of cold showers. Mary pushed a cupful across the table at me as I took a seat in one of my rickety kitchen chairs, and asked me if I felt better. I gave her an honest smile, and told her it was good to be back in the land of the living. Then I mumbled something about how it was good of her to be worried about me, but she really shouldn't.

"Well," Mary said, "somebody's got to take care of you."

"Yeah right," I said as I made a fast move to change the subject to something just a wee bit more comfortable, even if it was more painful. "How about you? How are things going with 'The Stud'?"

Sue was smiling at me, looking proud of me for being brave. She hadn't seen anything yet.

"You mean Chris?" Mary had that dreamy look in her eyes again, and no, I'd meant all the other studs in her life. "He's just great."

"Stop it!" Jake was at my ear again. "Just 'cause you're feeling lousy is no reason to take cheap shots at her."

Jake was right of course, but something was up here, I could feel it. My innocent little travel agent had a scheme of her own in the works.

"He's kind of lonely though, he's new in town and doesn't have any friends." She looked at me pointedly.

"What?" I said, more than a little quizzical, "you want me to hang out with the guy?" My voice even rose an octave as I said it. "No way! I'm a busy man, I haven't got the time to buddy around with any..."

Sue looked like she was going into shock across the table from me, as Mary said, "You're so busy typing all day that you just can't tear yourself away. Look, you guys drafted me for this little group, and I think he'd fit in too." She gave me a big-eyed look as she said, "Do it for me, Mel, please? As a personal favor to me." And that was the end of that. It was right about here that I realized that I was in big trouble.

After the ladies had gone home, I wondered if I had the fortitude to carve my own heart out with a rusty spoon.

"Life just isn't fair." I was still crying to myself, but thanks to my natural resiliency, I was beginning to see the humor in my present situation. Thank God. I think you normal people call it hysterics.

Jake was laughing outright at my anguish as I looked up from my now standard head-down position at my kitchen table. "You're getting exactly what you deserve, and you know it." He was off on yet another gale of laughter before I could answer the laughing mercenary.

Like I said, it's a good thing I've got a sense of humor. I started to chuckle as I watched Jake rolling on my kitchen floor. Soon I had joined him in his total lack of self-control. After several minutes of assorted giggles (and don't think you've done it all until you've seen a mercenary giggle), chuckles and snorts, Jake finally said, "A man can eat anytime, but a laugh restores the soul."

"Where did I hear that?" I asked him.

"A book somewhere, I think."

Chapter 8

Sitting in "our" booth at Mel's Diner, I was still trying to figure out exactly where it had all gone wrong, when Sue slid into the seat across from me. "So, how's it going, Romeo?" She was being sarcastic again.

I just gave her my "got the world by the tail with a downhill pull" smile, even though I was a long way away from feeling it, and settled back in the booth.

She just smiled back at me as she said, "Still in the denial stage, huh?"

"Exactly," I said, seeing no reason to deny the obvious.

"Are you going to be able to pull this one off?" Susan wanted to know.

I thought about it for a few seconds, running through all of my own doubts in my badly cluttered mind, and told her, "I can." Then I decided to give my nosy friend both barrels since she had brought it up. "I can because I love her so much; any way that I can make her happy is enough for me."

"'My life for the one you love,'" Sue quoted from Dickens.

I again leaned back into the hot vinyl of the booth as a smile came to my face. "I always loved that book, the winter of our discontent.'"

Susan's open palm hit the table with incredible force, jerking me back from the romance of the French Revolution.

"When are you going to get it? In this day and age, romance is the same as pathetic. Not to mention that this isn't some damn book we're dealing with here, Mel." She was mad as hell. "This is the real thing. If you don't tell her how you feel, she might never figure it out."

I reached out, and taking her hand, slowly and gently rolled it over until I could see the red soreness of her palm. Using the thumbs of both my hands, I rubbed her hand gently for a few seconds until I was ready to say, "I know."

The bell above the diner door rang as Mary entered with a (just like I'd figured) handsome young devil in tow. He looked to be about our age, somewhere in his mid-twenties, with sparkling blue eyes and a thick head of wavy blond hair (not a one of which was out of place). His face was Oh, Christ, chiseled like Jake's, and he flashed a truly sardonic smile as a beaming Mary introduced him into our group. He stood about six foot, was (gag!) broad through the shoulders and didn't even have the common courtesy to speak with a lisp or admit right up front to having several venereal diseases.

Susan got up and slid in beside me so the happy couple could share a seat. I somehow managed to shake his hand when he offered it, looking Mary square in her shoelaces as I told this guy how glad I was to meet him. His name turned out to be Chris Lucas, and his occupation was law enforcement. He had just gotten a job with what passed for a sheriff's department in this county, and had moved up here from the big city. It occurred to me that he had been here for a grand total of four days, and already, Mary was squirming up against him, with her arms wrapped around his waist as they sat across from Sue and I. And me? I hated him. Not just his guts either, I hated the whole package.

Chris was soon telling us about how exciting his job was, and how much he enjoyed saving the world from rampant crime. The world of law enforcement was apparently very exciting and romantic when viewed through the eyes of one Officer Lucas. Mary was watching him talk for Christ's sake, with that gaga look in her eyes. Sue, however, bless her heart, was beginning to look bored with the whole conversation. Mainly, I would guess, because she couldn't get a word in edgewise while Mary's new guy was talking about himself.

I nudged her leg with my own, as I put away what little pride I had left. "So, do you have any ideas about how to improve things in law enforcement around here?"

This question launched our newest friend into yet another diatribe of "what he thought." Mary smiled at me for just a second as I made my little effort to welcome this man into our "jungle pack"; even though Gray Brother wanted to gut him like a deer.

Please, stop me before I sub-reference again.

Susan even followed my lead and asked Chris more questions designed to put him at ease, not to mention making him look really stupid, but Mary didn't seem to notice. He prattled on for most of the afternoon, Sue and I simply putting all our suffering down to our friendship with Mary.

I was beginning to think along the lines of "what can she see in this guy" or maybe "it'll never last," neither of which had much of anything to do with my present situation. This was going even better than I had expected, and I was only ready to kill myself in the quickest way possible. True enough, this could've been the nicest guy in the world and my feelings about him would not have been any different, but this guy was really a grade A jerk.

I really wanted nothing more at this instant than to give up. Just slide back into my nice warm house and my nice warm bed. Standing on my front porch at six a.m., I faced a cold October morning on which even colder rain fell unmercifully. Turning to look at Jake, I said, "You're coming with me this morning, you owe me that much."

The hardened mercenary looked up at the overloaded clouds above and said doubtfully, "Well, okay..."

It was only a mile later in the freezing drizzle when I looked over at Jake and asked, "What are we doin' this for anyway? You know she doesn't even realize that I'm alive."

Jake thought about it for a second as we ran along (well, more like sloshed), and it occurred to me that the son-of-a-bitch didn't even have the common courtesy to be getting wet. Finally he answered. "Because we've got to show her that we don't give up, that you've got the strength of character to pick up and go on with your life..."

"What a load of bull." Even in the rain, it just wouldn't wash.

"Okay," Jake tried again, a little closer to the mark this time. "How about, if you fall all to pieces, she might figure out why."

Running in silence for a minute, I felt the cold penetrate my last layer of clothes before I said, "That, I can believe."

I was toweling off from a nice warm shower (my first in months, I might add) when I heard a loud knocking on my front door. I pulled on jeans and a sweatshirt and opened the door to find yet another one of my favorite people on the other side. "Sarcasm is a wonderful thing, it keeps you from going off the deep end," Jake said as Chris said, "Hey, Mel, Mary told me that you needed some company, so here I am." He walked into my house with that "this place is all right as long as I'm here" attitude, and sat down in my easy chair like he owned it.

I noticed that it had stopped raining, because my new guest still didn't have a hair out of place. Taking a seat on my couch, I forced a smile to my face as I said, "So what's up with you?" just like I'd been expecting him to barge into my home at any moment.

"Oh, you know," he managed to act like he was bored, "the usual things with a new town, new job." He grinned at me wolfishly. "New girlfriend. I'm sure you know how that goes, it's a miracle I can even walk." He laughed aloud as I finally caught his perverted line of thought. I managed to freeze an understanding smile on my face while my mind fought my body's basic urge to puke my guts out. I kept telling myself that this couldn't be happening, Mary didn't deserve someone who would talk about her like this to a nearly perfect stranger. She deserved somebody like, well, me.

By some miracle of my own free will, I didn't attempt to rip my new best friend's head off right away, as much as I wanted to. Although I doubtless spent the longest hour of my entire life sitting on my own couch listening to him rattle on and on about how great he was, there was one bright spot in my day. Eventually, he left.

As the door closed behind Chris, it felt like a huge weight had been lifted from my shoulders, until I remembered Mary. She had to know about this.

"You can't tell her, Mel..." Sitting in the easy chair that Chris had just left, Jake stopped when I turned on him.

"What the hell do you mean, I can't tell her?" I couldn't believe he was still making the rules up as we went along.

Jake stood to face me as he tried to explain, "Mary's in love with this jerk. If she's half the woman we think she is, when you start running this guy down, she's gonna tear you in half. There's no way she'll listen to what you have to say about her new lover. You're just going to have to wait until she's ready to hear what you have to say."

"Jake, c'mon..." I was arguing with myself, and losing already. "What if she's never ready? What if she marries this guy?" I was beginning to panic.

"Easy now, Mel," A mercenary trying to be soothing doesn't work very well. "She's not going to marry this guy and I'll prove it to you."

Looking at M.P.H. carefully, I asked, "How are you gonna do that?"

"Who is the most perfect person for Mary in the whole world?"

I took a long look inside and for once in my life; I came up with the right answer. "I am."

"That's right, Mel, you are. We've just got to give her time to see that. This guy is just a momentary distraction, a year from now she won't even remember his name."

I thought about that for a while and decided Jake could be right. "Even if he is just a bump in the road, what guarantee do I have that she'll end up with me?"

"You're the perfect man for her, right?"

"Right."

"Is she ever gonna find anyone who'll love her more, treat her better than you would?"

"No, never."

The mercenary smiled as he said, "What more of a guarantee do you need than that?"

You've just got to love it when your own imagination is there to give you a badly needed confidence boost.

Chapter 9

It occurred to me that I was spending more time than I should in Sue's pet store when the blue-haired postmistress started dropping off my mail there. "I'm sorry, Susan," I was in the middle of trying to explain, "it's just that I just can't go home."

Sue looked up from cleaning out a cockatoo's cage and said, "Now, why is that again?"

"Because he's always there." I couldn't bring myself to actually use his name.

Not quite understanding my dilemma, she had to say, "The way you feel about this guy, I wouldn't think you'd have any trouble running him off if you really wanted to."

"To tell you the truth, he's kind of like the old gum stuck on the bottom of your shoe. It would take atomic radiation to get rid of him, he's worse than a cockroach, and..."

"Well..." Sue wanted me to go on.

"And, and, I'm out of colorful metaphors."

Rolling her eyes, Sue said, "Thank God."

"Besides that, Mary wants me to be his friend, and I'll do that for her."

Standing up with a loaded dustpan in her hand, Sue looked at me for a moment. "Are you still thinking this is going to work?"

"I hope so." I didn't sound too confident, even in my own ears. "This whole thing started off bad and went to worse when she met Chris. But I can't give up now. I won't. And besides, she really is a good friend now, I don't need to pretend."

"Well," she said, "you sure are a persistent little bugger, and she should love you for that, if nothing else."

"It runs in the family," I said as I gathered up my daily junk mail and headed for the door. The chinch took a running leap to my shoulder as I told Sue over my shoulder that I would see her tomorrow, and pushed my way into the world. The sidewalk outside the pet store was covered with wind-blown leaves in the colors of red and yellow, letting me know that a blistering Montana winter was on the way, and that it would be a long, long time until spring.

Sure enough, when I reached the top of my driveway, there he was. The bright point of the situation was that Mary was with him. The only reason that was the bright point was that they had gotten past the "lovey-dovey" phase of their relationship, and I could actually stand to be around them as a couple without throwing up. Sitting on my front-porch step, Chris was in the midst of telling Mary that she should run some kind of special to help boost her business (where have we heard that before?). I waited a few seconds for Mary to come unglued and tell this bastard that her business was her business. I was, predictably, sadly disappointed in Life, Love and God in general. She just sat there with that silly, loving smile on her face that I'd give anything to see directed at me, and let Chris walk all over her. It occurred to me that she threatened to bounce me off the wall for suggesting the same thing, and wondered about the wisdom of falling head over heels for a woman who obviously just wanted what all the other women wanted. Someone gorgeous who would treat her like hell.

I shook my head, angry with myself for believing what I'd just thought. I'd let my own insecurities turn me against what I believed in, and it was my fault for letting it happen. I refused to lose sight of what I knew to be the truth. She was different. I knew it in my heart.

I pasted a nonchalant smile on my face, took that last step and said, "Hey guys, what are you up to?"

Mary started to speak and was cut off by her caring lover. "We thought that you might want to go out to dinner with us tonight, that is if you buy."

"Let me guess," I had to lash back a little, "it's still a couple of days until payday, and you and Mary had a date tonight, right?"

Chris just smiled that "the world loves me" smile and said, "Very perceptive."

Mary at least acted a little embarrassed as she hit Chris's shoulder, telling him to be nice. She smiled at me and said, "We really want you to come along with us, Mel. Who knows, you might have fun."

I was reminded once more that I was in deep trouble because I couldn't say no to her, no matter what she was asking of me.

Sitting at the booth that was formerly known in the annals of doomed love as "Our Table," I was really starting to wonder if I would survive this *meaningless* relationship with my sanity intact. I was wrong about them being over the "lovey-dovey" stage. Argh.

Mary managed to force herself to quit playing with that one damn lock of Chris's hair long enough to start a conversation.

"Have you met the new waitress here at the diner, Mel?"

It shouldn't be a real surprise that I could see this one coming from a mile away. I could actually feel the anger beginning to build. When would this woman start giving me what little credit I deserve? "No, I haven't, but I'm guessing you think I should."

She smiled across the booth at me as she said, "I just want you to have someone, Mel." She was still playing with The Idiot's hair. "You know, like me. Happy." She gave Chris another one of those puppy dog looks.

Ouch. Big time.

"She's a little babe, Mel," T.I. had to chime in, "I'm thinking about trying to get a little on the side myself." He winked at me so Mary couldn't see, to let me know that he was actually serious. I wanted to beat his bones to dust right on the spot, but I was afraid that Mary might take it the wrong way. The Goddess just laughed, thinking that he was joking, and told him that she loved him so much because he was so bad.

Huh?

I heard gum popping somewhere off to my right as someone with a very high pitched voice said, "Hiya, Mary, are you guys ready to order?"

I turned to find a bleach blonde waitress standing next to me, order pad in hand.

Mary introduced me to this new waitress, who went by the name of Annie. When the girl heard my name she immediately plopped down on the bench beside me, asking me if it was romantic to be a writer. The conversation was nothing but downhill from there. It's not that the girl was dumb or anything, just really not my type.

When Annie took our orders back to the kitchen, I gave Mary a level two dirty look as I said, "You told her I'm rich, didn't you?"

Mary shrugged her shoulders as she tried to answer without incriminating herself. "I might have mentioned that you make a comfortable living at what you do..."

"Never mind that for now," I was already on to my next point, "can you really see me with that girl? Did you really think I'd go for the blonde bimbo type?" I wasn't mad at her, I was mad at me for putting me here. Unfortunately, it didn't come out that way.

"Mel," she was doing a good job acting like she cared about me, "I just wanted..."

"Yeah, I heard you the first time," I stood up and threw a twenty down on the table to pay for the dinner that I couldn't stomach any longer. "You just want me to be happy, like you." I walked out the door without a backward glance. The dusting of powdery snow that had fallen to the ground while we were inside, let me know that I'd been patient too long, and that it might be time to move on with my life.

Someone was trying to break down my front door. At least that's what it sounded like inside my aching head. I stumbled up off the couch, nearly falling over the pile of empty wine bottles on the floor (well okay, two), and winced as the early morning light coming through the tightly shuttered windows hit the back of my eyes. I swam through my self-induced haze until the door appeared in front of me. Opening it made the bothersome heavy pounding noises stop, but they were immediately replaced by the high-pitched, and painful, tones of one irate little package of dynamite chewing me out royally. The worst part was I knew I really deserved it.

I'd made it all the way back to the couch and placed my aching head in my hands before Susan's voice actually started to form words.

"... only took her about ten minutes after you left the diner to dump Mr. Perfect off at home and show up on my doorstep, bawling like a baby."

I raised a hand in question, still a little foggy on the present subject, "Whoa, back up a minute. Did you say something about her dumping 'The Idiot'?"

Sue gave me a hard look. "Not with your luck, buddy. She's really upset, Mel, it took me most of the night to get her calmed down enough so she could sleep."

What had I done? The last thing I ever wanted to do was hurt her, and now I'd done just that. I had made her cry and I wasn't sure if my conscious would let me live with that fact.

"You didn't mean to hurt her, Mel, Jake was trying to help, we'll find a way to fix things, don't worry."

Apparently my conscious was more than ready for my troubles.

Groaning with two different kinds of pain, I said, "If she doesn't figure out I love her after this, she's got to be the densest woman since Lois Lane."

"Well, get ready to put on that blue suit. Studly, 'cause she doesn't suspect a thing."

I stared at her, mouth wide open. "You've got to be kidding."

She just shrugged her shoulders and said, "Nope, she thinks that you're just really mad at her for trying to set you up with that waitress. She has no clue about anything else. Your secret's safe with me, Clark," she added in a disgustingly cheerful voice.

"Thanks, Jimmy. Well, I was still being a little indignant about the waitress. "Can you see me with that ditzy blonde?"

"What's wrong with that?" Sue wasn't going to take my side. "She's really cute..."

"I don't care about cute. I've never cared about cute. I want... I need..." I ran out of gas in a hurry, trying to explain the thing that makes the world go round.

"Mary?" Sue asked.

One of those long, slow, painful sighs escaped me as I said, "Yeah."

It was a couple of days before I could gather up the nerve to apologize to Mary for the way I'd reacted at the diner. I stood at the door of the Midland Travel Agency with no little trepidation in my heart, a feeling that I was starting to get used to. I was going this one alone, without the chinchilla to soften the air between Mary and I. The little guy had really pitched a fit when I tried to leave the house without him, sounding a lot like Sue when she was chewing me out, and that was something I'd heard a lot of lately.

Pushing open the front door, I started to wonder if I'd ever stand in this lobby without being scared to death. Mary came out of her office to find me standing there with my hands in my pockets, and a forlorn look on my face. We just looked at each other for a minute or two, until I could find the words I wanted.

"Mary, I'm really sorry about the other day." It looked like tears were forming in the corners of her eyes, even though she was smiling at me as I stumbled through my apology. "I had no right to talk to you like that..."

I had to stop talking as she crossed the distance between us and threw her arms around me, laughing out loud with that graceful abandon I love so much.

Jake was with me in an instant. "Careful, Mel, don't read too much into this, you don't know what she's thinking."

"It was my fault for trying to set you up with that waitress, and you're apologizing to me?" She took a step away from me, tears of relief in her eyes. I unconsciously rubbed at my chest with my left hand, where it was still warm from contact with hers, and my heart was trying to tear free from my body. "No, it's my fault..."

Mary shook her head at me. "I promise I won't do that to you ever again." She gave me that puppy-dog look that could melt granite.

"Only if you accept my apology to..." I knew I was the one that was wrong, even if she didn't.

She nodded yes and asked, "Can we be friends again?"

Twinge. I hate the word friends, but at this point, I'll take what I can get.

It was my turn to give her a hug as I said, "We never stopped."

Slamming my back door as hard as I could scared the chinchilla into the bedroom, probably so he could hide under the bed with the dust bunnies. I stormed my way to my badly depleted wine rack and grabbed whatever bottle was closest to me. I was trying to rip the label off the bottle with my teeth when I heard Jake clear his throat behind me.

I growled over my shoulder at him in a voice harsh enough to scare even me. "Leave me alone, Stark. I don't want to hear it."

As usual, Jake cut right to the point he wanted to make. "You gonna let her turn you into a drunk?"

I was looking at Jake long and hard as the wine bottle shattered in my right hand. I guess I've been working out too much lately. I threw the chunks of glass into my trash can, and grabbed a towel to mop the wine from the kitchen counter. By the time I'd finished putting a bandage on my hand, I'd cooled down enough that I could at least talk to Jake, and tell him that I owed him one.

M.P.H. was sitting on my couch watching the sunset over the mountains as I came into the living room, still rubbing at my fresh bandages.

"Jake," I said, "thanks for what you did in there. I really appreciate it." I just didn't know what else to say.

He never even looked up as he said, "That's what I'm here for, buddy."

I sat down in my easy chair and joined the hardened mercenary in watching a spectacular sunset. Eventually, I said, "This woman is driving me crazy, isn't she Jake?"

"No, Mel, you're driving yourself crazy by holding back on your emotions. You can't do this forever. No one could. It has to end soon."

I made it through the night pretty well, when you compare it to the ones that came before, managing to catch a few hours sleep just before dawn. It had been a long time since I'd felt this way about anyone. I just lay in bed and thought about her for endless hours, going over everything she'd said to me, everything I thought she meant. I had imagined a thousand times what it would feel like to have her beside me. Not touching her, just close enough to touch if she wanted me to. Does that sound strange? Not the touching that counts, but that she wants, needs me to touch her.

Touching, isn't it?

Chapter 10

It was still pretty early in the morning when someone started knocking on my door again. The fact that the door opened all by itself, long before I got there, told me who my new visitor was before I saw his face.

"Hey there, Chris." I tried to sound happy to see him. "What are you up to today?"

Of course, he came right on in and made himself at home. "I just wanted to stop by and thank you, buddy." He was smiling again, and that made me nervous.

"What for?"

"For dumping that little blonde in my lap the way you did." I could tell from the start that I wasn't going to like this conversation. "She's even better in bed than Mary is."

My head was hanging low as I asked the obvious, "You didn't break up with Mary, did you?"

"Hell no." He was acting like he was surprised that I even asked. "Why would I settle for one when I can have two?" He was laughing like he was at the top of the heap, and I was finally ready to show him where he really stood. I was trying to think of what this might do to my relationship with Mary, and what it would do to her when she found out about The Idiot and The Bimbo, but I couldn't think very clearly at all just then.

"Go ahead." Jake was really there for me this time, giving me the green light that I hadn't expected to see. "Take him."

Chris got to his feet when I did, not really sure what I was doing. He was sure, however, after I hit him right on the nose as hard as I could. The big, tough man folded like origami, falling to the floor and making gurgling noises as I started to drag him out my door by his shirt collar.

"He's just a coward, a bully. He's not gonna have guts enough to do anything to you now." Jake was quiet for a second, then he said, "He is a cop though, he might want to press charges..."

I looked down at Chris while he just sat there in the dirt and watched the blood run out of his nose. "Oh yeah," I said, "one other thing. Go ahead and tell your cop buddies that you had your ass stomped by a scrawny writer. I'm guessing they'd get a kick out of that."

Shutting my front door behind me, I looked down at my poor mangled right hand, blood seeping from my split knuckles, and wondered if I had another roll of gauze anywhere.

I was digging through the medicine cabinet when Jake said, "That last part was great, I never would have thought of the scrawny writer bit."

I shrugged my shoulders and said, "I don't know, it just came to me."

As I walked out of the bathroom with my newly bandaged hand, I was thinking about what had just happened as I said, "We really handled that pretty well, didn't we? I mean, there was really no other way to go."

"Absolutely," Jake agreed with me for once, "Mary wouldn't believe you if you tried to tell her the truth, and he won't stop cheating on her, so you might as well make yourself feel a whole lot better, and at the same time get rid of that..."

I sat back in my easy chair listening to the mercenary's colorful adjectives and realized, I did feel better than I had in a long time.

I walked into town that afternoon, the beauty of the mountains around me matching the way I felt, and still all smiles over my new found career as a prize fighter. Sue took one look at me when I hit the pet store door and had to comment.

"What the hell happened?" She's just so ladylike sometimes it sends chills up and down my spine.

Talking through a super-wide grin, I said, "What-ever do you mean, Susan?"

"You look like the Cheshire Cat." Her eyes suddenly got as big as pie-plates. "Did you and Mary..."

"No! No, we didn't, and thank you for destroying my good mood." I gave her a partially angry look from my vast repertoire of facial expressions. "And what makes you think that every time I have a smile on my face, it means that Mary and I got together?"

"Just call me a student of human nature. Well?" she asked, "What happened?"

"You mean, Mary hasn't come in to talk to you?" I had figured that Chris would tell Mary so that she would never speak to me again, but if he didn't...

"We had lunch today," Susan answered, "but she didn't say anything out of the ordinary. What happened?" She was getting jumpy now.

My mind was in overdrive at the moment, trying to calculate all the possibilities of what I'd done this morning. If Chris hadn't told Mary yet, maybe he would be too embarrassed to tell anyone. "I can't believe that I might actually get away with it..." I mumbled to myself.

"WHAT?" Sue couldn't take much more of this.

"I can't tell you," I said. "It'll be better if you don't know if I have to go to court."

"Was he stupid enough to tell you about him and the blonde?"

I swear this woman would put Colombo to shame.

"How in the hell did you figure that out?" I was in shock.

Now it was her turn to be tight lipped. "Sit behind this counter all day, you hear things."

The trouble with her plan was that I knew her better than she thought I did. I just waltzed over and took a seat in one of her creaky wooden chairs, and waited. Eventually (about twenty seconds later) she broke down.

"All right, all right. One of the sheriff's dispatchers told me that one of the deputies had seen Chris leaving Annie's house at four in the morning a couple of nights ago. Then this morning one of the nurses from the clinic said that Chris had come in to have his nose set, and admitted that it didn't happen in the line of duty." She paused to take a breath. "So that leads me to think that Chris told you about Annie, and you punched him out. Right?"

I just stared at her for a moment, and said, "Amazing."

Susan just sighed and said, "One day I must learn to use my powers for the good of mankind, but until then..."

Laughing really is a lot of fun, ask the man who hasn't done much of it lately.

Things were pretty quiet for the next week or so, or at least they felt quiet after the way it had been going. I was still having lunch with Mary, but her "boyfriend" was conspicuously absent from these meetings. It wasn't hard to see that he hadn't told Mary about our little discussion, but that wasn't what worried me the most. He still hadn't broken it off with Annie (according to the rumor mill) and apparently didn't plan to. As if that wasn't bad enough, sitting across from T.G. in the diner, it started to come to me that she knew things weren't all roses with her and The Idiot. It wasn't really hard to get her to talk about it. Sitting in the diner for a cup of coffee later that week, she opened up a little more than I wanted her too.

"Something's wrong, Mel, and I don't know what it is." Mary was looking for another piece of the puzzle, an important piece that I was hiding from her.

"You know you can't tell her, Mel. She'll never believe it coming from you." Jake was still sure about that, and I was starting to wonder why, even though I believed him.

"He just seems kind of distant." She stopped for a second and looked at me, "I sound like an old cliché, don't I? You don't think he's..."

Sitting on the edge of my seat now, I was sure that she was going to figure it out for herself, and I was going to be there to see it.

82

"No, he wouldn't." Mary shook her head, crushing my hopes for the moment.

"I don't know, Mel, he just doesn't seem to be as interested in me lately." I gave her my patented "stupid" look as she paused. "You know, sexually."

Ouch and double ouch. She didn't even have the common courtesy to blush a little as she said it. But I did.

"I'm sorry, Mel," She was smiling at my embarrassment, but not laughing. "I didn't mean to rattle you that hard."

"Don't worry about it, Susan usually makes a big deal out of trying to embarrass me, so it's kind of a relief when it happens by accident." I wanted to talk about anything but what she'd just brought up in the name of casual conversation. I'm not saying that I haven't had my little fantasies about The Goddess, but a frank and open discussion about sexuality scares the hell out of me, and I'm not afraid to admit it.

I heard the door of the diner open, and almost cried out in relief when I saw it was Eric. I waved to make sure that he was on his way over to save me from further embarrassment. He slid into the booth next to me and said hello to Mary and I. "Sue is supposed to be here in a few minutes to eat supper, so you two better stick around," he said.

Mary glanced quickly at her watch and said, "Well, she'll just have to be mad at me. I've got to get ready for my date tonight."

She looked great to me and I told her that.

"Thanks, Mel, but Chris likes it when I get dressed up for him," T.G. said as she slid out of the booth, "so I'd better go."

Eric stood up to take her seat and she reached out and ruffled my hair as she walked by the end of the booth. I sighed my long-suffering sigh as I told her I'd see her tomorrow (big surprise there).

When she was gone, Eric reached across the table to hit me over the head with his baseball cap.

"What?" I wanted to know if I deserved that or not.

"Is there anyway you could possibly want her more?" he laughed.

"I really don't think I could," was my only answer as I "laid" my head down on the table with a bang that set the silverware to jumping.

I was in the same position, still pondering the wisdom of letting Mary go on in the dark, a few minutes later when Sue came in. "What did you do to him, honey?" she asked her husband.

"I didn't do anything," Eric answered, "he did it to himself."

As Susan sat down next to her husband, she said, "Mary?"

I whimpered aloud at the sound of her name.

"Mary." Eric confirmed his wife's suspicions.

"So let me tell her." Sue cut straight to the bone of the matter, just like always.

"No, if she doesn't find out for herself it won't do any good." I sounded like Jake now, and that scared me more than just a little.

"You're not going to let me tell her about Chris and Annie?"

"No way, Sue."

Her silence completely unnerved me. Looking across the Formica at her, I knew that there was no way that she was going to let this thing go so easily. I could tell from the look on Eric's face that now was a very good time to be afraid. Very afraid. Susan's eyebrows had furrowed, and her lips formed a tiny little "O" that denoted a form of concentration that she never uses until tax time, and I know I don't want the energy focused on me that she usually saves for the benefit of the IRS.

"Sue," I asked in a hushed tone of voice, "what are you thinking?"

She just smiled across at me and picked up a menu, "What looks good tonight..."

Chapter 11

It was about a week later when I heard a furious knocking on my front door. Muttering about getting a place further out in the country, I opened the door to find Mary standing on my step with her head down and a piece of notepaper in her left hand. She sounded kind of funny as she said, "Can I come in?"

"Sure." I stood to one side and watched her walk through the door and take a seat on the couch. She never looked up.

Mary was just looking at that slip of paper in her hand when I joined her on the couch, sitting at a carefully calculated distance. She handed it to me slowly and carefully, straightening out the wrinkles she'd put in it, apparently on the drive over.

I read it slowly and carefully, just like it had been handed to me. It was Chris at his most sensitive. He just told her that he had a better offer somewhere to the south of here and that he was taking the waitress with him, so Mary didn't need to write or call him anytime soon. Maybe he would get hold of her someday and thanks for the great time.

Mary's hands were crossed in her lap, and as I finished reading this "letter," I realized that tears were dripping from her face down to hands that were clenching and relaxing with each tear drop.

A strange thing. I had thought that when this breakup happened, I would be the happiest man in the whole world. Instead, it hurt me worse than I ever would have thought possible. All I could see was how bad Mary was hurting, and there wasn't anything I could do for her to make it go away.

Getting up from the couch, I made a short trip into the kitchen, returning with a bottle of wine and a box of tissues. Sitting at the same careful distance, I wiped at the tears as best I could, letting her know that I was there.

It was a few minutes and two glasses of wine later that she seemed like she was ready to talk a little.

"Why..." I was glad to see that Mary was going to start with the classics, "why would he do something like this to me?"

I clamped my mouth shut hard as Jake said over my shoulder, "Remember, she doesn't want a real answer right now. She just wants someone to listen to her."

He'd do something like this because he doesn't love you. He never did and he never will. I'm the one who loves you. Loves you more than life itself. Can't you see? I'd never hurt you, never.

"I mean, is there something wrong with me? Am I so horrible that he just couldn't stand to be around me anymore?" she asked.

You're perfect. You're perfect and any man that makes you doubt that for even a second should die a horrible death that would involve, at the least, a dull pair of gardening shears. I'd love nothing more than to spend the rest of my life making sure that you're happy. Please, please let me prove it to you.

"Is that waitress so much better than me? Maybe I'm not cute enough..." she went on.

Don't you see? He needed someone that he could outsmart, someone he could handle the way he wanted. You're too smart for that. Eventually, you would have seen through his tricks. You would have figured him out. You're smart and funny, and way past cute into beautiful. That waitress isn't even in your league. Why do you think I went crazy when you tried...

"I never want to date again."

Damn, never is one hell of a long time.

Reaching out to her, I allowed myself to put a trembling hand on her trembling shoulder. "You aren't going through this alone," I murmured. It was all I could think of.

Mary turned and gave me a look that was akin to gratitude. For an answer, she just slid over next to me, on my bargain basement couch, and pulling my arm around her shoulders, laid her head on my shoulder. She just wanted to be held. I just held her. S u s a n found us like that the next morning, Mary having cried herself to sleep sometime before dawn. And me? I wouldn't have moved if the world were collapsing around us.

I sat in the kitchen with Susan, listening to the shower run and hoping that my hot water heater wouldn't give out on T.G. We had bundled Mary into the shower as soon as Susan arrived, telling her that she would feel better after a hot shower and a clean set of clothes. Susan and I had searched frantically for something that would fit her, and Sue refused to let me deliver the T-shirt and jeans myself. So, I made coffee instead.

It turned out to be a good thing that Mary stayed in the shower forever, because Sue and I had a lot to talk about. I told her about the things you can find on your doorstep, and she told me about the nasty rumors that it takes to drive a sheriff's deputy out of town. No, I'm not kidding. Sue had started the rumor that Chris had his nose bloodied by an irate, five-foot, one hundred-pound husband of yet another woman that he was seeing on the side. She also gathered that his ideas for change and his personality had made him less than popular with his fellow officers. Those things combined with the other evidence of his personal habits were enough to make this old-fashioned town turn against him. It hadn't taken him long to get the message when he found that no one in town would speak to him except Annie the waitress. So, he quit his job without notice, loaded little Annie in the car, and left town. Hallelujah. Happy days are here again.

Susan had left to open the pet store by the time Mary emerged from my well-steamed bathroom. She sagged into a kitchen chair as I pressed a cup of coffee into her hands. She was quiet, and I was afraid that she might break into tears again any second. She had barely dried off enough to get into my clothes, her hair still dripping wet, so I picked up the bath towel from where she dropped it on the table, and slowly and ever so gently began to dry her dark hair. Her reaction was immediate and gratifying, letting me know that I hadn't gone too far. Her shoulders lifted, and I could see the smile on her face in the reflection from my kitchen windows. When I had finished, she told me that she was going to go home to bed. I walked her to the door, a hand tentatively placed around her waist. She stopped at the door and, putting both arms around my neck, kissed my cheek.

"Thank you for being such a good friend, Mel."

Damn, that word stings. Not as much as it used to, but it still hurts.

"I'll get these clothes back to you as soon as I can," she said.

"Don't," I said, "it feels kind of nice when someone swipes your T-shirt. You know?"

She looked at me for what felt like forever before she said, "I know."

I somehow managed to enjoy my walk home from the pet store that day in the beautiful scenery that surrounded me, the familiar gravel road crunching under my "almost new" Reeboks. I sorted through my mail as I walked, and found the usual credit card applications, Greenpeace and PETA sending me more pictures of rabbits with acid dumped on them (does that bother anybody else, or am I the only one?), and the other normal stuff. At the bottom of the stack was a letter from The Barnes and Noble Publishing Company of New York City.

I tore open the business envelope, and fished out the check payable to yours truly for the yet to be written, latest installment of the Axeman series. There was a standard issue form letter from my editor, Rick Jamison, and a hand written note from the same. I read slowly as I walked up the driveway. He just wanted to know if I was still alive, being a long while overdue for the book that the enclosed check paid for. It had taken him several months to convince the accounting division that I could be trusted with an advance, and he asked that I please not let him down. And I should call him when I can, signed your buddy, Rick.

Knowing that if I didn't call him now, I never would, I walked into the house, picked up the phone and immediately dialed the publishing house. After an embarrassing conversation with the switchboard operator, I found myself speaking to one Rick Jamison, Head of Action Adventure Editing at one of the most prestigious publishing houses in New York.

"Hey Mel, old buddy, old pal, how are things in the wilds of Montana?" Rick asked from his olive drab cubicle in the basement of a forty-fifth street brownstone. (What? Like I'd have some high dollar publisher?)

"Life sucks out here, Rick." At least I managed to be up beat. "How's New York?"

"Just like always." He sounded as happy as I was. "Looking out my window, I can see a drunk peeing in the middle of the street. Oh, excuse me, 'homeless person.' Is there a politically correct way to say 'peeing'?"

I laughed aloud as I imagined Rick looking out his street-level basement window, and answered with, "That would 'bladder evacuation.'"

"But you?" he asked, "why does life suck in the middle of what I've always thought must be heaven?"

I sighed into the phone. "Women."

Rick crowed like a rooster on the other end of the line. "You sound totally whipped, guy. Does she have you running in circles?"

"Completely."

There was utter silence on the other end of the line, and then I could actually feel the heat from the lightbulb over Rick's head. "Mel, I've got it."

I knew I'd hate myself for asking, but, "Got what, Rick?"

"Who usually writes books on how to meet women?" he sounded really excited. That's bad. Ask the man who has experience with excited editors.

I sounded really confused. "I don't know, maybe doctors or

somebody with a degree?"

"No," I wasn't surprised by his answer, "the people who know how to pick up women are too busy picking up women to write any measly book."

"Your point being..."

"You've got time on your hands, why don't you write a book on how to pick up women?"

This was his big idea? "Rick, I don't know a damn thing about picking up women, my track record on this is really bad. Trust me on this."

"Neither do those guys whom write those books, wasn't that the point I just made here?" he didn't sound dissuaded by my argument. "Look, Mel, we both need this, you don't want to spend the rest of your life writing pulp action adventure, and I don't want to spend the rest of my life in this basement. Try it, would you? For my sake at least, try it?"

I sat in silence for a long time. How is it that the people around me always know what buttons to push?

"All right," I said, "I'll try it."

Sitting once more in front of my word processor, I felt like I had been away for twenty years. I stared at the LCD screen for nearly an hour before I realized that I had no idea where to start with this project.

"Having trouble?" Even Jake's intrusion came as a welcome break at this point.

Pushing my worn out office chair away from the desk, I turned to Jake and said, "No, not really. I just don't have the foggiest idea of what I'm doing."

"That's never stopped you before." Jake was slipping.

"Oh, that's funny," I couldn't let him get away with it, "and so fresh too..."

"Sorry, I guess I am a little off today, but that's your fault as much as it is mine."

Spinning in my chair like a three-year-old, I stopped to face Jake again. "Why don't you just blame everything on me?"

Jake even looked tired to me, his iron back having a definite sag to it, his eyes bloodshot. "Your center is way off today, trying to do something you don't know anything about. Can we go back to another Axeman book?"

I looked at Jake in shock, I'd never heard him ask for anything in the all the years that I'd known him. An alarm started to ring somewhere in the back of my mind, it was starting to feel like Jake had been too nice for way too long.

It was then that I started to realize that I really felt like hell. It just felt like everyone had been after me lately, Jake didn't want me to write this book, Susan didn't think things were going to work out with Mary, Rick wanted me to drag us both out of obscurity with a talent I really don't believe I possess, and most importantly of all, Mary had wanted me to be friends with the bastard who had everything I wanted in life and didn't care that he had it, and now, who knows what she'd want next. Everybody in my life was against me in one way or another, and I had only been hurting myself with all of the drinking I'd been doing lately. I had just about decided that there was no way that I could take much more of this when I heard the sound of another voice in the confined space of my den.

"Don't listen to him, Mel, he's just trying to run you down." It was a soft, feminine voice that was badly out of place here.

I whirled around in my chair to find an absolutely gorgeous brunette seated on the edge of my desk. I made the mistake of trying to talk right away and found out that my brain was still too busy gawking to handle any form of speech. It was Mary, but not quite. There were a lot of differences between the two, I realized as my mind slowly began to kick back into gear. She was about my height and was kind of slender in a wiry sort of way, and where Mary's hair was dark, hers was jet black and held off of her forehead by a headband ala Rambo. Her clothes mirrored Jake's, a worn pair of blue jeans and a black tank top, even though I can't remember Jake ever looking that good. But it was her eyes that drew my attention. They were a strange color that hung between blue and gray, almost the same shade as the morning mists I'd run through on the mountain. With a shock I realized, they were Mary's eyes. There was more though, this woman just looked more dangerous, more like...

"No, no, no..." I started to bang my head on my desk slowly at first, gaining speed and force with every thump. She looked like a female version of Jake.

"You guessed it, handsome." This lady mercenary gracefully crossed her legs (why are women always so graceful?) and continued, "Your mind created me the same way it created Jake, and for much the same reasons."

"Which would be?" I hated quizzing the various figments of my imagination, but I didn't figure I had much of a choice at this point.

"Because you need help." She was different from Jake too, intelligent charm is what it felt like to me, instead of his macho self-confidence.

Jake had been silent for too long. "Careful, Mel, you never know what she might tell you..."

Andy rolled her eyes at me (now, how did I know that her name was Andy?) and said, "Oh come on, Jake, I'm the honest one here. You're the one who comes from the lying side of his brain..."

I sat, completely engrossed, and watched two parts of my psyche battle it out. The gloves were definitely off when Jake told Andy to go back to whatever Freudian nightmare she came from. Andy blasted back with something that amounted to what Jake could do with the average Freudian nightmare (it sounded physically impossible to me). I decided to let them fight for a little while just to see how Jake would fare against this new kid on the block.

Eventually they fought themselves to a standstill, not just a truce, but a real stalemate. At the same instant, they both noticed that I was just sitting there, watching them yell and scream.

"What?" they said simultaneously.

"Just waiting to see who survives."

Jake just gave Andy and I a disgusted look and stormed out of the room.

Andy just looked at me for a second before she said, "What do you want to talk about?"

Stunned doesn't even quite cover my condition as I said , "What do you mean?"

"You sent Jake packing so you could be alone with me, didn't you?" She seemed to take this for granted. "And since you are a disgustingly habitual gentleman, I'm assuming you want to talk about something."

"What makes you think I got rid of Jake?" I still wasn't getting it, and the implications of what she'd just said were making my head spin. "Not to mention that your estimation of me is a little too high."

"You don't know then?" She seemed perplexed.

"Don't know what? Jake controls me, not the other way around."

Andy was struggling to put this into words: "You are what makes our friend Jake pop in and out of your life; when you need him, or on some level, think you do, there he is. When you don't want him around any more, he goes away. So when you sent him away just now, I assumed it was because you wanted to talk to me." She flushed a little as she said, "If you want to do anything else, you've got the wrong fantasy woman..."

"Hold it, hold it, hold it," I interrupted her just before she could really embarrass me. "This sounds like a load of B.S. to me Andy, and by the way, how do I know what your name is anyway?"

"That part's simple, Mel, your mind created me, so you got to name me." She was beginning to take on the attitude of a kindergarten teacher with a stubbornly slow student, which was a lot better than her previous attitude.

"But why did my mind kick you out all of the sudden? I mean, it's not like I didn't have enough troubles with Jake already..." I thought I might be able to get something out of her I never could get out of Jake. He'd always told me that I had just needed him, and there he was.

"Your mind made me to balance Jake out in your conscious mind. We're two different parts of your personality. He's the macho, love 'em and leave 'em, everything bad you put in your books."

"And you?" I knew I'd hate myself for asking.

Her answer was simple, "I'm going to help you with this new book, and I'm the one who's going to get you Mary Byrd."

Chapter 12

She was right too, about the book anyway. I sat in front of my old word-processor and cranked out a good twenty pages that first day, outlining my previous failed attempts at the manly art of wooing women, and why I thought they had all failed. With Andy's supportive help, I had a strong idea of where the rest of this book was going to go, and how I was going to get it there. It all depended on my relationship with Mary.

I spent a lot of time wondering about this new kind of imaginary friend and why she should be so different from Jake, but at the same time, so much like him. I guess the obvious answer would be that they should be somewhat similar, both having sprung from my slightly neurotic intellectual loins, so to speak. Also, having come from, as Andy put it, different parts of my brain, they would be basically different.

Jake is supportive too, I guess, in a macho way. Running a guy down could be a manly man's way of helping your friend if he's got a basic confidence problem. Sound's kind of iffy to me, but then I'm no doctor. I'm sure that if I ever get low enough on cash, I can sell myself to the highest bidder for psychiatric testing. If I can get them to believe me.

I guess the point is that I now had My Personal Heroine to balance out My Personal Hero.

The holidays were almost here. Isn't that kind of like saying would somebody take my life, please? It's a fact that's only made worse by the fact that I'm living in one of the most beautiful places in the world to spend Christmas. That is of course, if you can stand being buried up to your butt in snow for five months out of the year. But once you get past that, it really is beautiful. Sometimes, when I'm standing on Main Street, I really expect to see Jimmy Stewart come running down the street screaming at the top of his lungs (does anybody else wish that Ted Turner would give that show a rest?).

I know it sounds really corny to say this, but the whole town just kind of comes to life about this time each year (is there a song in that? Nah...), with the people decorating their shops and homes with every light bulb in town. You can call me old-fashioned if you want to, but my personal favorite has always been the antique nativity scene that they put up in front of the courthouse every year. It probably helps add to my "crazy old man" reputation when I stand among the tall pines of the courthouse lawn for hours on end as the snow falls around me and simply look at that old stable. I didn't really care if the people whispered behind my back as I stood there for all those hours with only the depth of the snow and what little feeling I had left in my toes to mark the passage of time. Every once in a while the town's current crazy old man, the courthouse groundskeeper, would come by and carefully remove the snow from the carved wooden figures. Sometimes we would talk, but mostly he would simply nod to me as he walked by. I guess there is some kind of recognition among kindred spirits.

It's not that I'm mental or anything, I just like to look at that old nativity scene because it kind of takes me back to when this time of year wasn't quite so lonely.

You see, each year my folks would drag me down to the Christmas pageant that the Chamber of Commerce held in our home town every year and sign me up for whatever part was left on the night of the big show. So, you can guess that I never got to play one of the cool parts like Joseph or the Angel. Nope, I always ended up crouched down under a smelly old sheepskin going, "baabaa" (and on cue I might add).

Looking back on it all, I was glad that I did, seeing the happiness that it brought to Mom and Dad. It's kind of sad because now when I remember those days, I can see that they were already getting too old to keep up with a child my age. I guess they were around sixty then, ready to retire, but they really couldn't because of the child that came to them so late in their lives.

All of the good things about my childhood seemed to be wrapped up in that one thing. Not the whole nativity scene, but just the foot long, poor lost little lamb that always sat in the far corner, forgotten by everyone but the old groundskeeper and me.

Enough about that, it's not Christmas yet.

In the middle of all this, an idea came to me for the next Axeman installment. As they usually do, this one came at a rather inopportune moment, running down one of my mountain trails that would make the average billy goat stop and think "Now, why did I want to be here?" I managed to make it all the way back to the house with my idea intact, and didn't even bother to shower before throwing myself at the word processor with the energy of a man possessed.

Andy wandered in as I finished with the first chapter, and started trying to read over my shoulder. I shut down the IBM and told her to mind her own business, but I was already too late.

"You're putting me into the Axeman series?"

To say that she was a little excited by this prospect would be yet another of the world's greatest understatements.

"I guess you deserve it for all the help you've been to me lately, and besides, I still owe Jamison another Axeman book." I tried to downplay it as much as I could, because, to me at least, it was really no big deal.

Andy snorted at me. "Are you trying to make me feel special or what?"

Imaginary friend or not, she is a woman...

"You are special." I had decided that it was time to take a new direction. "None of this would be possible without you, and I owe you for that."

This brightened her mood considerably. She threw her arms

around my neck and gave me a good squeeze as she told me thank you. Andy pushed away from me to give me a stern look as she asked, "You're not going to make me into some kind of a pyscho-slut are you?"

"I can only write you the way you are, and you're no pyscho-slut."

She smiled at me and turned to walk away as I added, "At least not until the full moon."

I made a mental note to remind myself of something as I lay on the floor trying to decide if I could still feel the rest of my body. Never make a lady angry. That goes double for a lady mercenary.

Slogging through the fresh snow on my way to deliver the freshly finished newest installment of the wildly successful Axeman series to the post office, I hoped that I hadn't cost Rick his job by taking so long in getting it done. Included in the manuscript was a letter asking him not to send me anymore advance checks until I sent him the books. To tell the truth, I wasn't really sure if I would write anymore or not.

Over the sound of the snow crunching under my boots, I heard Mary calling my name. I stopped and listened for a second. Liking the way she says my name doesn't make me crazy, does it?

Turning around on the sidewalk, I watched my (recently promoted to) best friend manage to zig zag her way up to me through the slush and ice on the sidewalk without falling on the pavement.

"What's up?" I asked, having found out in the past that if I don't keep my end of the conversation to a minimum, I might say something more than Mary wanted to hear.

"Can I walk along with you for a little while?" She didn't seem to want to look me in the eye, and it was giving me that old familiar sinking feeling in the pit of my stomach.

"Uh oh." I could tell that something was coming, and I found myself hoping she hadn't found another damn boyfriend. "Sure, you can come along if you want. I'm just going down to the post office, what can I do for you?"

Mary laughed at my ability to tell when she needed something. She quickly took my pro-offered arm when she stepped across a patch of ice, but held on even after she was on firm footing again. "You always know, don't you?" she asked.

"If it makes you feel any better," I answered, "you do manage to slip a good one by me every once in a while."

She was quiet for a second before saying, "I need a favor, Mel..."

"Oh, come on." I thought I could throw in a plug for myself. "You know that you can ask me for anything." I even managed to say it so she wouldn't think about it too much.

Mary looked at me now, and I could see that this was important to her, whatever it was.

"It's a big favor, Mel. A really big favor."

We rounded the corner in front of the old, brick courthouse and stopped in front of my all-time favorite Christmas decoration.

She turned to face me as we stopped, and I couldn't tell if it was the cold making her cheeks turn red or something else.

"It's my family, Mel."

"Are they all right?" Now she was scaring me.

"No, no, they're all fine. It's just that..." She stopped in mid sentence and started kicking the snow at her feet.

I thought that I'd better just wait this time, and before long she continued. "They all think I've still got a boyfriend."

"You never told them about Chris?"

"I told them that he left. But I also kind of told them that I'd met somebody else."

Unable to resist, I asked, "Oh yeah, when do I get to meet him?"

She really slipped one by me as she said, "Actually, he is you." Huh?

Andy was with me instantly, telling me, "Let her talk, Mel. We don't know what she really meant yet."

"How about a little faith here?" It just kind of slipped out.

"Faith in what, Mel? What are you talking about?" Mary was looking confused now.

My brain must have hit overdrive in that instant because I came up with, "Have a little faith in me, would ya? What's your plan?"

Relief flooded her face as she did that wild abandon thing again, throwing her arms around my neck and giving me a squeeze. We won't talk about the effect this was having on me, let's just say that I was feeling all right.

Mary released me and grabbed my arm again, steering me on towards the post office as she said, "I need you to act like you're my boyfriend when I go back home for Christmas. All the tough stuff, you know, meet the family, Christmas dinner..."

I looked back over her shoulder at that lamb and asked, "The Christmas pageant?"

"Sure, if you want." She was smiling again at me. I like that. "What do you think?"

Shrugging my shoulders, I smiled back at her and said, "Sure, why not?"

"You have no idea what this means to me, Mel." She gripped my arm tight for just a second. "I really appreciate it."

Looking at her with a deviant smile, I said, "You know that your mom's gonna love me, don't you?"

"Yeah, I know it."

Chapter 13

"You're gonna do what?" Apparently, volume beats tact in Sue's book.

Repeating what I'd just said, "Spend Christmas with her family in New Mexico."

"As her..." Sue let the question hang.

"Oh yeah, didn't I tell you that part?" I let her stew for almost five seconds before I finished, "As her boyfriend."

"She figured it out? You two finally..." She jumped just a little too far ahead again.

"No, and quit doing that to me. Her family thinks that she has a boyfriend and she needs me to fill in. That's all. Nothing else."

Sue just looked at me for a second, obviously thinking hard. I really hate to give her the chance to do that, there's just no telling what she might come up with.

"So you think that this will give her a chance to see how you would act if you really were her boyfriend. Not to mention the fact that her mom is going to love you." She still amazes me sometimes.

"That's pretty much it, Sue." I shrugged my shoulders and sat down to take the heat.

I was pretty shocked when she just smiled and said, "I'm impressed, Mel. I didn't think you had it in you."

"What do you mean?"

She just shook her head at me and asked, "When are you going?"

Letting that one pass, I answered, "The weekend of the

eighteenth."

"I hate it when people celebrate Christmas before it's actually Christmas, you know what I mean?" she said.

Shrugging my shoulders in an attempt to sidestep an argument, I said, "It was the only time that all of her family could get together."

"All of her family?" Sue was smiling as she asked.

Swallowing the lump in my throat, I said, "Uh huh, all of them."

"I know that having the family together is important, I just wish that it was as important to everyone else as it used to be. Back when you did anything you could to be together on Christmas Day." Susan looked as sad as she sounded.

Hoping that a change of subject might help, I asked, "So, when are you and Eric getting together with your families?"

"The weekend of the eighteenth."

Oops.

"So," she said after a few quiet seconds, "I'm going to have a party on the real Christmas Eve, you want to come?"

"Wouldn't miss it for the world."

Jake and Andy were waiting for me when I walked through the front door, stomping my feet to get the snow off. The two of them almost pounced on me, trying to pry information out of me about what I had planned.

"I know you too well," Jake started, "to think that you're going to let this opportunity slip on by."

Andy pushed Jake out of the way, saying, "He's not going to take advantage of the situation, he loves her too much for that."

I just looked at them for a second before I said, "You two are leaving me quite a bit of room in the middle here. Are you sure you don't want to change the rules while you've got the chance?"

"Nope," Jake said.

"We trust you." Andy was in this boat too.

"All right. All I'm hoping for is the chance to show Mary what it would be like if I were her boyfriend. She needs to know what it feels like to have someone that cares about you, someone that will treat her..."

"Like a Goddess?" Andy must have a little bit of Sue in her somewhere.

"Yeah," I said, "something like that."

"I'm impressed, Mel," Jake said as he clapped a hand to my back, "I didn't know you had it in you."

I know that I jumped and stared hard at Jake for a second, almost asking him what he meant. It didn't take me to long to remember that Jake was my way of reminding myself of what Susan had started and not finished. I knew that she was upset with me for letting myself in for this and that she thought I would be taking advantage of Mary by doing what she wanted me to do. But what Sue didn't know yet, was that I would do whatever it took to get close to T.G., and that was something she would have to learn on her own.

"Did you mail the book?" Andy wanted to know. It still amazes me how different from Jake she is sometimes, asking me for information that she should already know. Maybe that's a part of her.

"Yeah, I did."

"Do you think Rick is going to like it?" She was almost hopping up and down.

I smiled at her. "I'm sure that he will. Jake was long past due for a partner, you're just what the series needed to pick it up."

It was Jake again. "Then why are you thinking about ending it?"

It's a hell of a deal when your own imagination pulls something like this on you. I sat down in my trusty easy chair and took a deep breath, trying to think of a way to explain.

They were both just standing there looking at me, wondering why I would stop writing about them, stop giving them new lives. "It's...just that I've been distracted lately, and I'm not writing enough to keep the series going. Rick will have to dump the Axeman if I can't turn out books more often than I have been."

"Nope, that's not it, Mel, and you know it." Jake again cut to the center of the problem. "It's more like, the books aren't enough of a challenge to you. The truth is, they never were, but this woman, this travel agent, she's brought things out in you that I never thought were there. You need to write something other than this pulp action stuff, you could write classics if you tried."

Andy wrapped her arms around me from behind and rested her chin on top of my head. "We're a part of you, Mel, and we just want the best for you. It's all right."

"Thanks for understanding, guys." I told them, "It really means a lot to me, but I haven't decided what I'm going to do with the series yet. It might go on forever, I just don't know."

"She's changed you a lot, Mel." Andy said, "You've grown a lot since this whole thing started, and something tells me you've got a ways to go yet."

"Andy's right, buddy," Jake said. "That travel agent is good for you. You're really going to be hard to talk to if you ever get her to realize that you can be good for her."

"That'll be the real trick, won't it? Whether or not she sees it in me. I hope that will happen soon."

"Maybe what you want will be under the Christmas tree?" Andy asked.

"I just hope that Santa Claus loves me."

Well, here I sit. Staring at the back of a really big guy who was also on the way to Santa Fe. The bad news was that I was going to be eating my knees for the entire flight. The good news was that Mary was still feeling guilty about asking me to do this, which equated directly to her being really nice to me for the whole trip. That is, when she wasn't drilling me on the finer points of her family.

"Okay then," she asked, "my cousin Joey does what for a living?"

Cousin Joey had gotten a divorce a few months ago, had a five-year-old daughter named Maggy, and worked as a, "Teacher at Winnipeg High." I told you I love this woman.

"What does he teach?" Mary was smiling.

"Uh..." Damn.

Now she was laughing. Wasn't there something about women loving men that can make them laugh? I think another important part of that cliché should be that she is laughing with you, not at you.

"It's okay, Mel," she said, "you're doing great, I can't remember anyone ever trying this hard at something for me before."

Looking out of the window at the ground far below suddenly became a lot easier than looking at my traveling companion. Why would she say something like that if she didn't mean it? Didn't she realize what it meant? I just kept telling myself that this weekend might be *it*, that she might finally understand that I'm the perfect man for her. If I stopped for a just a second and thought about what I was doing, the stewardess would have to tell me to remain in my seat instead of trying to shove myself out one of the windows. I hate it when somebody that passes out foam pillows and barf bags has to use a firm tone of voice to maintain control.

"Sorry," Mary was saying, "I didn't mean to embarrass you."

"Huh?" I turned back to her with an innocent expression on my face. "Did you see that bunch of geese that flew by the window?"

"Good cover," Andy said.

"Oh yeah, she's gonna buy that." Jake was being himself again.

She didn't even nibble on the line. "It's just that, I'm not used to men who would do all..." she waved a hand around us, "this, just for me. It seems like the only guys I'm attracted to are the ones who wouldn't lift a finger for me."

"Well," I managed a little laugh as I said, "it's a good thing that you're not attracted to me then, otherwise you'd have to change all of your rules."

"Yeah," Mary said as she leaned back in her seat to get some sleep, and not finding that comfortable enough (or heartbreaking enough for me), she slid over, actually laid her head on my shoulder, and wrapped both of her arms around my left arm.

"It's a good thing..." and she was asleep.

I had to scrunch my neck to get a decent look at her sleeping face, and I was not disappointed. You guessed it, she even slept gracefully. Not to mention the fact that by the time we landed in Santa Fe, I had one hell of a crick in my neck.

When we parked the rental car in front of the little house just outside of Coyote, New Mexico, I had a hard time tearing my eyes off of the tremendous scenery of the Nacimento Mountains as Mary gave me one more look and asked, "Are you ready?"

Taking a long deep breath, I said, "Sure, how about you?"

"Mel." She ignored my question in yet another attempt to make me nervous. "I can't tell you how much I appreciate this."

Mary was looking at me with those killer eyes again, and I was having one hell of a time concentrating on the task before me. Finally, I shook myself and answered her. "Why don't you wait to thank me until after this is all over, okay?"

"Okay." She agreed.

As we opened the doors to get out of the tiny Ford that Mary had reserved for us at the Santa Fe Airport, the screen door on the little house that was nestled against the hillside banged hard against the peeling white of its wooden siding. The Goddess met the lady that was running towards her at full speed half way up the sidewalk. All I could do was smile as I watched the tearful reunion that was going on in front of me. (Where is Sally Jessy when you really need her?) When the tear-fest broke up, I got my first look at Mrs. Byrd. You want to know something funny? In that first second, I would've sworn that she looked just like Radar O'Reilly's mother, but the more I thought about the likelihood that she was a pretty fair depiction of what Mary was going to look like in her later years, I decided that she was a very attractive (in a matronly way) lady.

"Mom," Mary was saying, "this is Melville." As she lead her mother to me, T.G. didn't look a bit nervous, but I figured that was okay, because I was nervous enough for both of us.

"Well, I'm pleased to meet you, Melville." She extended a hand for me to shake after wiping it quickly on her floral print (no kidding!) apron.

Taking her hand in a carefully calculated handshake, I said, "Please, ma'am, just Mel is fine." It's never too early to be polite, mother used to say.

Her face lit up as she took me by the arm, leading me toward the house as she said, "Oh my, and he's polite too!" See, I told you.

I stopped Estelle before we reached the house, telling her that I should get our luggage out of the car now to save a trip later. T.G. told her mother to go on in the house before she got cold and that we would be inside in a second. I watched her totter off to the house, and thought that I heard her chuckling the whole way.

Throwing open the trunk and grabbing my duffel bag and Mary's three suitcases (some clichés really are true), I was a little surprised to feel Mary's arm around my waist. At least I didn't drop the suitcases.

"You're doing great so far." She said, "That ma'am thing was just perfect."

"Thing!" I was trying to be indignant. "That was no 'thing.' My mother always said..."

"It's never too early to be polite." She finished for me.

I just stared at her until she shrugged her shoulders and said, "It shows."

As we walked up the sidewalk to the house (well, she walked, I struggled like a sherpa following a crazy white man to the top of Everest), Mary told me that the rest of her family would start arriving later on that night, so I had plenty of time to get acquainted with the most important member of her family. According to T.G., if I could get "Mom" to support me, the rest of the clan wouldn't have any choice but to like me. Oh yeah, no pressure.

My only thought as we walked into that house was, could this be any more classic? I stopped in the doorway and stared like an idiot as I tried to take it all in. Lattice-topped cherry and apple pies were cooling on the sideboard of a china hutch that looked like it had probably been brought west in a covered wagon. The oak kitchen table was covered with every kind of home baked cookie that I could imagine, and the scent of cinnamon and nutmeg promised that there was a pumpkin pie baking in the oven.

We made a little small talk as I began to feel the suitcase handles cutting furrows into the flesh of my hands. Estelle was stirring a gigantic pot of something on the stove that smelled amazing, which she stopped doing when she saw that I was just going to stand there with my chin resting on my chest, holding all the luggage, until she showed me to our rooms.

We followed her down a narrow hall to a room that was decorated in the motif of "teenage girl."   Mary didn't even give me a chance to make a comment, saying, "Yes, it's my old room. Do you like it?"

"Love it," I said with no small enthusiasm. (What am I, stupid? No, don't answer that.)

Estelle was headed for the door when she said, "I'll just let you kids get settled in..."

"Um..." I thought I was nervous before, "Ma'am? Which room is mine?"

"Oh, I thought you kids could share this room since the house is going to be so crowded. Besides that, I may look old, but I remember what it was like to be young." And with that she was off to the kitchen again, leaving two shocked "kids" in her wake.

"What kind of mother lets her daughter sleep with her boyfriend?" I was sitting on what I took to be a footlocker of some kind that was covered in flowers, with my head in my hands.

"She probably wouldn't have if you hadn't been so damn polite!" Mary said in a hushed voice. At least it was easy to tell that she was as shaken by the current turn of events as I was. "I can't believe that she would do something like this. She wouldn't even let me hold hands on the front porch when my dates brought me home in high school."

"Did you have a lot of dates in high school?" I was suddenly distracted.

"Who cares, Mel! We've got other things to worry about right now." She was walking around the room in really tight circles, and I found myself noticing that there was a definite worn path in the rug where she was pacing. There must have been a lot of teen-angst going on in this room.

"Wait a minute," Mary stopped in mid-stride, "we're adults here. Aren't we?"

She got a funny look from me as I said, "You could sound a little more certain."

"What I mean is, why can't we just share the bed?"

I didn't need Jake to warn me not to get excited this time, I was getting used to keeping my wildest hopes and dreams under control. I tried to look thoughtful as I realized that this woman really trusted me. I'm not sure whether that's good or bad, but it's true.

"We could," I decided to do the 'make her laugh' thing, "if you promise not to take advantage of me."

It worked. When she stopped laughing, she said, "Don't worry, your virtue is safe with me."

So it was settled. Mary and I would be sleeping together, and I wasn't sure if I was in Heaven or Hell.

Chapter 14

I really think, looking back on it all, that it was the tenth time that I asked Estelle if there was anything that I could help her with, that cemented me forever into her good favor. I know, because it was shortly after that when she grabbed my cheek and said, "I love this boy!"

All I could do was blush and give Mary my "I told you so" look. Of course, this plan was not without its drawbacks. I had already fed the dog and the cats, taken out the garbage, changed a couple of light bulbs, replaced the drive belt on a vacuum cleaner that gave every indication of being older than I was, and I was sure that I would now be sent out to clear a field or split rails. I wasn't too far off.

"Actually, Mel." Estelle was still stirring that pot, and even though I would have thought it was impossible, it was smelling better than before. "If you want, you could get the wood ready for the fireplace tonight. The woodpile is in back and there is an ax in the tool shed."

No problem. Mary trailed me outside and sat on the back step munching on a cookie pilfered from her mother's table while I started to split wood.

"You sure do work hard when you're on vacation." At least she was smiling when she said it.

"It's the least I can do for her, considering the fact that she is letting me sleep with her daughter." I couldn't resist that one, and I was guessing that Mary's sense of humor was still working.

She just laughed and said, "I really do appreciate what you're doing.

It's made this so much easier to let her think that I finally found a decent guy. You know, you're the first guy I've ever brought home that she's liked."

I almost chopped off my own foot at that moment. I was having visions of a white Christmas spent at the emergency room before a quick peek proved to me that all my tootsies were still intact. "It's a good thing you didn't tell me that." I said, "I don't think I could handle that type of pressure."

I split one more log before I said, "That can't be right. You surely brought home somebody that she liked."

T.G. had a kind of thoughtfully blank look on her face as she answered, "Nope, never once did she like any of my boyfriends. Not until I bring one home who isn't really my boyfriend, and you she likes!"

I thought about that for a second before walking over to the back step and taking a seat beside her. It should be obvious to everyone but Mary that her mother had impeccable taste, and was only trying to protect her daughter. The trick would be getting Mary to accept that.

"I know, I know," Mary said as I settled down next to her, "she's just watching out for me, and I always bring home guys that treat me like..."

Yeah. How do you get someone to accept something that they already know?

"But still, you would think that she could have picked one to like out of all the men I've dated over the years."

All the men?

"How many of those men treated you as well as you deserved?" I asked, well aware that I was on very thin ice.

Mary thought about it for a while and came up with the right answer. "None of them."

"Then your mom just wants you to find someone that will treat you decent, and that's easy for me to do because, after all..."

T.G. threw her hands in the air as she said, "I know, I know. We are sleeping together."

I was just looking out over the little valley below us, and wondering at the snow-covered beauty of this place when I heard Mary say, "It's beautiful here, isn't it?"

It even scares me sometimes, how much we think alike.

"Absolutely, I can see why you had to open your agency somewhere else. The people would never want to take a vacation from here."

She snorted aloud and said, "Oh yeah, and the Montana mountains are any better. If I had any brains, I'd open an agency in Pittsburgh, or Cleveland. But no, I pick scenic Browning for my venture into the business world."

Mary was quiet for a second, long enough that I thought she was done with this topic, until she said, "I had to leave."

I wanted to tell her that she didn't have to say anymore, but something told me that she wanted to.

"I did a lot of dating here, but always the type of guy that Mom didn't like. The ones who didn't treat me right, the ones with worse problems than I had. It was beginning to feel like I would never find 'the guy,' at least not here.

"I'd been working in a travel agency here in town since getting out of college, and I decided that it was time to try it myself. Mom was really sad to see me go, but I think she understood why I had to. I hope she did anyway."

She took a deep breath and smiled at me again. "So, my search for the perfect man has brought me across the country, apparently to you."

It was on her lips, but it wasn't in her eyes.

I laughed aloud so she wouldn't see the pain in my eyes and put an arm around her shoulders. "Then we're both in big trouble, aren't we?"

Wiping the corners of her eyes, she said, "You will be if you don't finish chopping that wood, since you volunteered."

Once again, no problem.

Once the wood box beside the ancient stone fireplace had been filled, The Mother of The Goddess sent her daughter into town for some more baking supplies, insisting that I stay so that we could have "a nice little visit." We talked about almost everything as we sat at that old oak table that I doubted had come from a garage sale. I was valiantly attempting to steer the conversation away from my alleged relationship with her daughter, but I soon realized that I was dealing with a master.

She had apparently decided that it would take a frontal assault to breech the subject she wanted. "So, how long have you been in love with my daughter?"

Somewhere, I'd once heard that no great gain ever came without chance. "Since the first moment I saw her."

I think that one bought me two rungs on the "Mom ladder," not to mention a plate of cookies and a glass of milk.   "So when do you think that she's going to find out that you do?"

Huh? I may have bobbled it momentarily, but I did not drop the ball. "She knows, Estelle. We have a very good relationship, we talk about these things all the time."

"Oh come on, Mel, you don't have to play that game, she's gone to town."

Huh again. When did she turn into Dr. Ruth Doggy Dog? "What game? Mary and I have a very solid, loving relationship."

"Quit it, son, I know that you're just acting like she's your girlfriend for my benefit. Or is it for her benefit?" She was waving her hands in that exasperated gesture that I've seen Mary use before, and did she just call me son?

"So the gig is up, huh?" I asked.

"Yes it is, and you haven't answered my question yet. Does she know that you love her?" Now she was doing some kind of Colombo thing.

"No she doesn't, but how is it that you know about all this?"

"I'm her mother, I know things about her that she doesn't know. Besides that, I'd have to be blind and stupid not to see the way you feel about her. That's not something you can fake." She even acted like Mary when she was being smug.

I thought about it for a second and asked, "The kitchen window was open?"

"Just a little," she said, holding up her thumb and forefinger about an inch apart, "it cools the kitchen off when the stove makes it too hot in here."

"I thought so," I said. "So what are you going to do?"

"If it's so important to her that I think she's seeing somebody, we'd better just leave things as they are. She probably wants her brothers to think you two are a couple."

"Her brothers?" I asked.

I never even heard anyone behind me. All of the sudden, I found myself pinned against the kitchen wall by two very large men who were now attempting to crush my shoulder blades together. Estelle was yelling at them like they were ten years old, "Mark, Matthew, don't hurt him!"

The little one's (he was probably only six foot five) jacket gapped open right in front of my eyes and I found myself face to face with a Bianchi shoulder holster holding what looked like a Beretta .40 caliber semi-automatic. Great, they were either gangsters, or...

"So, you guys are cops, huh?" I squeaked.

"This is Mary's boyfriend, Mel." Estelle was behind these two guys somewhere, still pitching for me. I wasn't sure if they were going to let me go once they knew whom I was supposedly sleeping with. But they finally did. I realized then that I was going to have to have words with Mary over this little surprise, making me memorize her family tree for three generations and leaving out the incredible hulks...

"What were you boys thinking? Attacking Mel like that?" Estelle wasn't done chewing them out.

"We were thinking, 'strange guy in the house with Mom' is what we were thinking." This was the big one's comment on the situation. I learned something today, if you can't see the top of a guy's head, it's really hard to gauge his height.

"Good instincts guys," I said as I was attempting to straighten my clothes, and was surprised to find that my voice was starting to come back. "It's all right Estelle, I hadn't had my ass kicked yet today. I'm actually kind of relieved to get it out of the way."

"What are you doing calling her Estelle?" The little one seemed to take offense to that fact.

"Well, for now." I took a seat at the table again, and gave their mother a broad wink. "We're working our way up to 'Mom.'"

The big one (who had to be Matthew, even though Mary had forgotten to mention anybody's sizes, or occupations, or the fact that they even existed) laughed and took a seat beside me, saying, "I like him. Anybody that is that big a smart ass is okay by me."

"Thanks Matt, I appreciate that."

"What do you do?" the little one (Mark) paused for a second before he added, "Mel?"

Estelle answered for me. "He's a writer, a very successful writer."

"Anything I would have read?" Mark was still not giving up.

"No, probably not..." I still hate telling people that I write cheesy action books.

"He writes the Axeman series." Now I was wishing that Estelle would just be quiet for a while.

The reaction was immediate, and loud. "You write Jake Stark? You write the Axeman?" Matt leapt up and slapped me affectionately on the chest. I just kind of lay on the kitchen floor for a second until the room came back into focus. Matthew apologetically helped me back to my feet, dusting me off (yet another scary moment for me) and setting my chair upright again. As I sat back down, I noticed that Mark was now smiling at me from across the table. I wondered if it was the fact that I made a decent living or if he just liked seeing me get the crap beat out of me, or maybe it was both.

"Well," Mark said, "at least this one's got a job, sort of."

Bingo.

"I love those books," Matt was saying, "everybody reads them down at work. How is it that you know so much about all the things that are going on in the world? I mean, a lot of the stuff that you write about isn't exactly common knowledge."

"I do a lot of research and I read *Solider of Fortune*. Other than that I've got a friend that helps me out a little every now and again."

"Somebody federal?" he asked, an expectant look on his face. Who am I to disappoint somebody so damn big? I gave Matt a smile and a broad wink.

"I knew it, I knew it! I told all those guys that you were in with the feds! Wait 'til they hear that you're dating my sister." Matt was really excited now, and even his brother was starting to loosen up a little, faced with the fact that I wasn't bumming my way through life using Mary like an ATM card.

It was then that Mary got back from town with another pound of cream cheese for her mother. When she came through the door, I stood up, letting her kiss my cheek when she had finished saying hello to her brothers, and giving her my chair at the table, since it was the last one in the room.

Mark was still giving me something that looked a lot like Mary's "what the hell are you up to now" thing that she does so well, as I leaned up against the counter and asked Estelle what she planned to make with the cream cheese.

"My grandmother always used to make cream cheese cupcakes in the old country, so it's a family tradition to make them every year at Christmas." Estelle said as she started getting ingredients out of the pantry.

"It's also always been a family tradition since the old country to use store-bought vanilla wafers to make them with," Mary added with a smile.

As her mother turned back to face me, I could see that she did in fact have a box of vanilla wafers in her arms.

"It's a well known fact, child," she said to her daughter, "that the Nabisco company was started in the old country over two-hundred years ago by a little old widow woman."

The kitchen erupted into laughter with the punch line of what was obviously an old family joke. For the first time in a long time, I started to let myself feel like a part of a family again.

By the time Matt and I finished getting the fire started after dinner, I wanted to stay here forever. The house was full of people, and for the first time in my life, I didn't mind being a part of a big crowd.

"You're not a part of this fam...oomph!"

"Shut up, Jake! Enjoy yourself, Mel, you deserve it."

Thanks, Andy.

"Having fun?" Mary asked as she leaned over my shoulder, joining me for a second as I crouched in front of the fireplace, watching the flames as they started to eat at the wood that I'd split that afternoon.

"More fun than I've ever had in my life," I told her.

When I turned to face her, Mary's eyes held a concerned question.

"Later." I promised as I reached out and touched her cheek gently, some part of me using the fact that half her family was watching us as a reason to touch her, but most of me was touching her because she wanted me to, and didn't know it yet.

Hand in hand, (God did that feel good) we walked to the brightly decorated Christmas tree, and spent a lot of time with Mary leading me from ornament to ornament, each one with its own story. Here was the one she'd made when she was in the first grade. There was the teddy bear that she'd bought her mother for helping her with the high school Christmas pageant. In the very center of the tree, in the most conspicuous spot, was a beautiful antique crystal ornament. I asked Mary about it.   "That one I ordered for us when I was twelve. It came all the way from New York City, and I had to save my money for a year to get it. I just wanted the nicest things for all of us, but one ornament was all I could afford. Even with my baby-sitting money and whatever odd jobs I could scrape together, I still ended up having to borrow some of the money from my dad..." She grew sad for a moment, and for some reason, I didn't push her. "It looks nice though, doesn't it?" she asked.

"It's beautiful," I answered her, but I wasn't looking at the Christmas tree.

I sat down on the floor with my back to the warm hearth, and was intensely gratified when Mary snuggled up next to me by the heat of the fire. At this point, I really didn't care if she was acting for her family or not, I was just happy to be here, and I guess it showed.

"Mel," Estelle said from her glider rocker in front of the fire, "you don't look like you could be any happier."

I tried to look thoughtful for a moment as every eye in the room shifted to me, but I couldn't keep my idiotic grin from coming back to the surface. "You're right, there's just no way that this could be any more perfect. I feel like I'm in a Norman Rockwell painting."

Appreciative laughter all around greeted my observation. Cousin Eddy even noted that if we weren't reminded of how perfect our lives are, we tend to forget it. Mary squeezed my arm tightly to tell me thank you again, even though she really didn't need to. I really was having the time of my life.

"Are you two sure?" Estelle asked as Mary and I made for the door, on our way to the Christmas Pageant that Mary had promised me.

"We'll be fine by ourselves, Mom," Mary told her, "you just visit with everybody, we won't be gone very long."

"All right," Estelle said, "if you really want to go all by yourselves..." She gave me a subtle wink as Mary drug me out the door.

As we pulled up to the town square, it felt to me like I really had come home again. Mingled in the crowd that ebbed and flowed around us, little kids dressed as angels, wise men, and even a lamb darted in between the people who had come to see them, usually pursued by a distraught mother. I was just standing there watching it all with my patented lopsided grin on my face, when Mary slipped her arm around my waist (for the second time today I might add. It's kind of pathetic when you count those kinds of things) and asked me how long I planned to stay in one place.

I just smiled at her as we walked to the tiny stage that the town had built just for the pageant. As we found a place to sit among the crowd where we could watch, I told Mary that this town couldn't be more perfect.

She nodded as she said, "You're right. Growing up, I thought that all towns were this perfect at Christmas time, but when I left here, I realized that wasn't true."

Her voice had grown sad as she spoke, so I tried to make her feel better by sharing my theory about the town of Browning and Jimmy Stewart.

Mary laughed and threw her arm around my shoulders as she said, "So you think that we're spending Christmas in the two best towns in America?"

I looked around us again, and said, "I really do."

We had a few minutes before the pageant began, so Mary decided to start a conversation to kill the time.

"Why did you want to come to the Christmas Pageant anyway?" Subtle, isn't she?

"You don't like going to the Pageant?" I thought I could turn this around, but I was dealing with her mother's daughter.

"No, I didn't say that. I asked why you wanted to go to it."

I took a long deep breath, wondering how much I should tell her.

"Tell her..." Andy said in my ear.

Mary nudged my shoulder with her own, saying, "Tell me."

"When I was little, my folks used to take me into town and put me in the Pageant every year. The only thing was, they always waited until the last second so I ended up with the part that no one else wanted."

The little lamb for this year's pageant chose this moment to make a break for freedom, at least, I think that was what he was doing as he crawled underneath my chair. I let this certain distraught mother pass us by before I exchanged quizzical looks with Mary and pried the young boy of about ten out from his hiding place.

"What's the matter?" I asked him.

He pushed the lamb outfit back from in front of his eyes and said, "I'm in a lamb suit and my mother wants me to get up in front of the whole town. What do you think?"

It became obvious to Mary and I both that things had changed a lot since we were this kid's age. I moved over one seat and put him in the chair between Mary and I, trying to stifle my laughter. The costume had fallen down over his face again, making both Mary and I break out in laughter. Mary controlled herself first and waved me to silence, afraid that we might do further damage to this boy's fragile psyche.

"What's your name?" I asked him.

"Justis," he said. He must have seen some serious doubt in my face because he added, "I know, I know, but my dad's a lawyer. I've even got a sister named Miranda. She gets to be an angel, and I have to play a sheep."

"So you don't want to do it, huh?" Mary asked him.

"Not really." He was a little dejected under all that fake wool. "But if I don't my mom'll be really disappointed."

I nodded in agreement with him and said, "Yeah she will, and I'm guessing that you're not the kind of guy that would let your mom down."

The lamb's head sunk a little lower as his chin hit his chest. "I guess not. But why do I have to be the dumb sheep?"

Mary looked across at me and shrugged her shoulders.

"You're a writer," Andy said, "say something to the boy."

I took another deep breath and waded in with both feet. "Do you know the story of the Baby Jesus?"

He looked at me from underneath that hood and said, "Who doesn't?"

"Well, what you might not have heard was what happened after the baby was born. It was cold in Bethlehem at that time of year, and since they couldn't build a fire in that rickety old stable, Mary and Joseph were worried that it would be too cold for the newborn Christ child. It was then that one of the animals came forward and lay down beside the child, its thick coat keeping the child nice and warm. Which animal do you think it was?"

"Are you trying to tell me that it was the lamb?" To say that the kid was a little bit skeptical would be a huge understatement. I thought about checking him for ID, more sure now than ever that he was really a thirty-year-old midget.

Instead, I told him, "Absolutely. D'you wanna take a stab at who told me that story?"

This time, he just shrugged.

"My dad. He told me that when I said that I didn't want to play the lamb in the Christmas Pageant because I was sure that I would die of embarrassment."

He just looked at me for a second before he said, "You had to play the lamb?"

"Yep. I did it because my mom and dad wanted me to, and I didn't want to let them down."

That little kid just kind of shook his head at me and said, "All right, you made your point, I'm going..."

He started to walk towards the stage and barely made it three steps before his mother swooped down on him and whisked him away.

I kind of smiled as I watched him go, until I got the funny feeling that somebody was watching me. I turned slowly to find Mary just looking at me. Talk about nervous. I self-consciously wiped at my nose, asking her in my ever so drawn-out style, "What?"

"That was why you wanted to come tonight? Because you miss being a kid?"

I almost fell out of my chair. How could she figure out something that obscure, and not see the way I feel about her? I guess love really is blind. Or is it blinding?

"How did you know?" It was too late to be cool about it anyway.

Mary shrugged her shoulders and turned to the stage, saved from having to answer my question by the entry of the angel choir. For the next few minutes, we were both lost in the telling of one of the oldest stories, told to us by young children. I started wondering if anyone had ever thought about what that meant. I shook my head at the idea, telling myself that I was too young to be sounding like an English teacher talking about the double meanings in *A Tale of Two Cities*.

The little lamb came out right on cue, and even let out his "baabaa" with perfect timing. I think Mary and I might have cheered louder for him than his parents did. When it was all over, the two of us walked back to the car, Mary's arm again linked with mine. I heard something behind us that made me turn and saw the lamb in his father's arms while his mother was kissing his cheek. The sound I'd heard was the two parents telling the boy how proud of him they were. Justis spotted me from his perch and gave me an enthusiastic wave. I waved back at him before I stepped into the car, happy that he had gone through with the pageant.

I started the car, letting it warm up for a second before I decided to remind T.G. that she still owed me an answer.

"I guess it just made sense," she said. "Even as good a writer as you are, you couldn't have made up that story about the lamb on the spot, so it had to be true."

"You're right, it happened just like I told him it did. My dad didn't want Mom to be disappointed in me for chickening out of the Pageant, so he told me that story. It worked then too. I went through with it, and I was really glad that I did later on."

"You know what else?" Mary asked with a mischievous smile on her face.

"What?"

"You're going to be a great dad someday," she rubbed my knee as she added, "if you can ever find a wife."

I even said it out loud. "Ouch."

Chapter 15

The bedroom door shutting behind Mary had a kind of a cell door sound to it as we faced the lone bed together. Uncomfortable was really an understatement and it looked to me like the bed had actually shrunk in the course of the afternoon.

Mary cleared her throat nervously (good, then I'm not the only one) before she said, "You were going to tell me something that you didn't want to. Remember?"

"Oh," I said, caught flat-footed by her reminder of our earlier conversation by the fireside, "I was kind of hoping that you'd forget about that."

"No chance," she said as she plopped herself down on the bed and patted the mattress next to her for me to join her. Funny thing, when she did that, Mary wasn't being coy or anything. It was just kind of...charming.

I sat down with her and said, "It's nice to have a family around you. If you've never been without one, you don't know how great they are. I haven't had a real family since Mom died, and I guess that I never realized how much I missed it until today." That was my first lie to Mary. I always knew how much I missed having a family around me, I felt it every day when I woke up in that empty little house on Mamut Road. No one can live alone forever and still be happy with the way they are.

"I'm sorry, Mel," she said. I thought for a second that I could see a tear in her eye, but I decided that it must just be the light. "I didn't know that this would be so hard on you..."

"Hard on me?" I shook off the feelings of sadness, and put a smile on my face. "I told you, I'm having the time of my life." Or at least, I would be if it weren't all a lie, if we were really together. Can't you see how good we are together? The family wasn't all I was talking about when I said it was perfect.

"Besides, I told you that your mom would love me."

I never even saw the pillow coming and I'm not sure I would have ducked if I had.

Mary stormed off the bed in mock anger, heading for the adjoining bathroom and saying, "I'm getting ready to get some sleep."

I put on shorts and a T-shirt while she was gone and spent several moments wondering what Mary might wear to bed. I was kind of ashamed of myself for thinking about something like that, and I was also ashamed for not thinking about it sooner. I never claimed to be normal. T.G. came back to the bedroom wearing pajamas that were about two sizes too big, satisfying both parts of my battered psyche with the ultimate coverage broken only by some heavenly sent gappage occurring in just the right spots as she climbed into bed. Wow and double wow.

I turned off the lights and crawled into bed beside her, careful not to touch her as we lay next to each other in the dark. The last thing I wanted to do was invade her "space." We both were quiet for a few seconds before Mary burst into laughter.

"We really act grown up, don't we?" Mary sat up in bed with a shocked look on her face, reaching out to poke me in the shoulder. "Oh no! I touched you!"

"Ack! You gave me cooties!" I responded and gave her a poke to the right shoulder in my own defense. The following, well, poke-fest, was not of a sexual nature. It was just good clean fun.

Eventually, we were all laughed and talked out and she said goodnight, falling asleep with her head on my shoulder for the second time today. Oh yeah, I was going to get a lot of sleep tonight. I stared at the ceiling, wondering about the things that had put me in this single bed with the woman I wanted more than anything in the world asleep on my shoulder. I thought about the way her touch on my body made me feel, the way her complete trust in me was letting her sleep like she had not a care in the world, and most of all, how my own rampant stupidity kept pushing me deeper and deeper into Mary's life, but not as what I most wanted to be. When I couldn't think about all that any longer, I started planning a dream house for the two of us. I bought every piece of wood at the lumberyard myself, and nailed the boards in place in my mind. Somewhere around building the second story, I finally fell asleep.

A heavy pounding at the bedroom door made me jump and look at the clock. Six a.m. Time to get up anyway, and two hours of sleep should be enough for anyone. I was trying to slip out from under Mary's arm without waking her (a sound sleeper, that girl) when the door burst open and two huge men pushed through the doorway.

"Mary?" I said in a tiny voice, "help."

The two men advanced on me in the darkness, their faces hidden in shadow, and lifted me bodily over their heads and made for the door with the somewhat bewildered prize. From my upside-down vantage point, I could see Mary only burrowing deeper into the warm quilts as I thought I heard her say something about "family tradition."

As I was being carried through the kitchen, I waved (not so nonchalantly) at Estelle, who was standing by the stove with a big smile on her face and a cup of coffee in her hands, apparently waiting for my return. Out the back door and into a pile of fresh fallen snow I went, and I'll tell you that it didn't take me long to test the temperature of that snowbank with my ass. Trust me, it was cold.

I was hopping around in front of the kitchen stove as Estelle was trying to press the aforementioned cup of coffee into my hands. The two monsters that had done this to me were collapsed in the corner with laughter, and after thinking about it for a minute, I decided that the better part of valor was a good sense of humor, and a long life.

"Get dressed, buddy." Matthew slapped me on the shoulder. "We brought you a shotgun that should work for you just fine, so let's go try and get a few pheasants."

Sipping from my coffee, I answered with, "I don't have a license, boys, and the last thing I want to do is break the law in the presence of two fine officers. You two go ahead though, I'll just stay here with the women folk." Not to mention the nice, warm stove. Mama Melville didn't raise any weak-minded children.

Mark was waving a piece of paper in front of my nose. "You've got one now. Mary made us get it for you so we'd have to take you along whether we liked you or not."

A lightbulb went on somewhere. It may have been dim, but it was definitely there. "So Mary's in on this little tradition, huh?"

"In on it?" Matt asked. "It was her idea to begin with."

The boys were waiting for me when I finished getting dressed, stomping into my boots as I came back into the kitchen, but I asked them to hold on for a second longer. I walked out the back door and scooped up a handful of the cold, tingly stuff. Not saying a word to anybody, I walked back through the house, careful not to spill any snow on Estelle's floors. Stepping quietly into Mary's bedroom, I pulled the covers off of her and spent just a second looking at her serenely sleeping face before I dumped the snow right where the tops and bottoms of her wonderfully too big pajamas gapped to expose her rather attractive belly-button. I whipped the covers back over her and said something about "family tradition," running like hell for the door as the screaming began.

Her brothers were just standing there with blank looks on their faces as I ran between them, headed for the kitchen door at Warp Three.

"I wouldn't just stand around here, boys..." I heard Estelle say to her sons. She didn't have to tell me though, I was already long gone.

We rolled to a stop on the edge of a field that appeared to be covered in weeds and about six inches of fresh powder. The two brothers spent the next few minutes explaining about cover for the birds we were hunting and the local farmer that had always let this field grow up with just the kind of stuff that they liked. I was ready to go at it, but I found that the two guys by the doors were simply sitting there, staring out the windshield.

"What's up, guys?" I wanted to know.

Matt gave me a funny look and said, "Can't you see the sunrise?"

Shocked that these two huge, rough men would spend time looking at the sun, I took a look myself, and forgot why we'd come out here. The sun coming up over the foothills was turning the whole landscape an unbelievable shade of red. The frost on the grass was alive with a fire that was beyond description, and the steam rising off of the small stream that ran along the edge of the field rose to mingle with the low lying fog that was even now beginning to burn away.

We sat in silence until the bottom of the sun cleared the mountains to the east, and Mark said, "We'd better get at it, they'll be sitting so tight we'll practically have to step on 'em to get them up."

Climbing out of the truck as quietly as I could, I almost laughed when they handed me an old, double-barreled twelve gauge, without a buttstock pad or anything.

"What are you guys trying to do, kill me?" I asked.

Blank looks again. "Mary said you didn't know much about guns so we thought you could use..."

"I may not shoot much, but even I can tell that this is going to hurt like hell. If you guys are making me use this, I get the credit for all the birds we get, okay?"

They just kind of grinned at each other for a second before saying, "Deal."

It was truly a beautiful day as we trudged along in the snow, watching our breath frost the air in front of us. I was doing great until I actually had to shoot. I was moving the gun to my shoulder as three birds burst from cover almost right in front of me. At least I've got a chance of hitting one, I thought as I put the bead on the center pheasant and pulled the trigger. Now, what my two new best friends hadn't told me was that due to an unfortunate accident involving a pickup door and the very same gun I was using, both barrels would fire when one trigger was pulled. For those of you who don't know, that's about the equivalent of getting into a shoulder-punching contest with Mike Tyson (after prison). The good news was, I got all three birds. The bad news was that I was once again staring at the sky. At least this time it was a beautiful blue, but for the second time today, my butt was getting wet.

Matt's face appeared above me as he asked, "Is he making snow angels?"

Mark joined him and said, "Nah, I think he just got tired."

They helped me up yet again, brushing the fine, white powder off of me as best they could with me doing all that moving around. Why couldn't I hold still? You try it with a couple of grizzly bears bouncing you back and forth between them.

"Hey, hey, that's all right, guys." I winced as I tried to rotate my shoulder, but picked up those three birds without too much trouble. Thinking about the beautiful animals that I carried as we walked back to the truck, I felt proud of myself, providing for this family that had so recently adopted me. It was important to me, and it made me feel good.

"We'd better get these back to the house so Mom can get them into the oven," Mark was saying as I listened to our feet crunching in the snow and pondered, well, the meaning of life more or less.

"Just wait until you taste her herbed pheasant in mushroom gravy, Mel." Matthew wrapped an arm around my shoulders as he tried to impress upon me how tasty these birds would be when Mama Byrd finished with them.

"The turkey will be going in about now, getting the dressing ready for the oven too," Mark was saying with a kind of dreamy look in his eyes.

I did a quick check on my watch, and not being much of a culinary artist, I decided to ask, "Is the turkey going to get done?"

Matt nodded his head and said, "Sure, it's a wild bird that we took this fall. They don't take as long to cook as a store bought bird; there's not as much fat so it cooks faster."

I nodded in agreement as Mark continued with the menu list, "The cream cheese mashed potatoes and green beans almondene. Broccoli casserole and honey biscuits with homemade jelly."

Matt had to add, "And she always has a big pan of homemade cinnamon rolls and a pot of coffee in the morning, when everybody else finally gets up."

I'd heard just about enough. "Then what are we waiting for?" I wanted to know.

They both looked at me and said in unison, "Christmas."

Ooo, that smarts. A direct blow to the less than funny bone. While their timing was good, I thought they needed some fresh material.

I cleaned those birds for Estelle the same way I'd been doing everything else, making up for my lack of knowledge in the subject with sheer, unbridled enthusiasm. They went into the oven with the turkey at just the right time, according to the cook. So, I joined my hunting partners in a cup of coffee and a roll, and listened to them telling yet another family member the story of how I had reversed the usual order of falling down and going boom.

Straightening out their twisted version of the tale for about the tenth time, I suddenly noticed Mary leaning against the doorjamb. She was giving me that cold glare that she saved for special occasions, and it frightened me just a little.

Everybody in the room had heard the story of the snow in the bed, so they all kind of scooted their chairs away from me, or took a big step back, leaving me all by my lonesome in the middle of the kitchen floor.

"Now you have to admit," I said, always figuring that the best defense is a good offense, "you did deserve what you got for letting me in on your little family tradition."

She was still just looking at me, frightening me more than a little and prompting me to say, "Well, okay. You don't have to admit it, but it's the truth."

Mary shrugged and walked across the floor to me, saying, "I guess you're right, and it was worth it to see you hauled out of the room like freshly killed game." She slid on to my knee, since it was the only open seat in the room, and put both hands around my neck. I didn't even flinch as I felt her own handful of snow go down the back of my shirt. Mary was still smiling into my eyes, and all I could do was smile back as the room erupted into laughter as the snow dribbled to the floor. Did I mention that I love this woman? And her family?

After I had gone outside to rid myself of some of Mary's latest gift, I resumed my seat and Mary resumed hers. I was not surprised to find that my cinnamon roll had been pilfered and my coffee pretty much gone. I wasn't that disappointed, either. She threw an arm around my shoulders and mumbled an apology around the last bite of my roll, but another magically appeared in its place. As she sat in my lap and helped me finish off the second roll, I started to feel guilty for not telling her that her mother had figured out our little game. Should I tell her? What am I, stupid?

What followed soon after was one of the all-time greatest Christmas dinners in history. Do you remember the Pilgrim's Feast? Or maybe The Feast of Trumpets? People were starving at these events compared to the massive face stuffing that went on at the Byrd house. The guys hadn't been lying about the quantity or the quality of the food that was carried from the kitchen to the dining room table. We put every leaf we could find in that table, but it still threatened to be too small as dish after dish was brought out and deposited on its groaning surface.

Wild turkey, my pheasant and ham dominated the center of the table and they were flanked by seemingly unending rows of casseroles and baskets. It was a real challenge for me not to stuff myself, but to instead just take a little bit of everything. You guessed it, I stuffed myself with everything.

A break in the ensuing coma occurred about two hours later when Mary's face appeared between the ceiling and me. It seems like I've been doing that a lot lately, but I really didn't mind when the view was this good.

"What's up?" I asked as I stretched and fluffed the couch cushion that I was using as a pillow.

"We'd better get going if we want to make our plane," she said.

Aw, already? Getting to my feet seemed to take a major effort on my part as stuffed as I was, and because I didn't really want leave. We said our good-byes to the other folks that were strewn about the room in the same condition that I was in a moment before. Mark and Matt both shook my hand and told me that they'd look forward to seeing me again, since it would give them someone to knock around.

Estelle followed us out to the car, drawing me to the side as Mary put her last bag in the trunk.

"Thanks," I told her, "for everything. Including keeping our secret."

She just gave me a hug and said, "I'll see you soon, Mel."

Giving her a less than confident look, I said, "I hope so Estelle, I really do."

She had a self-assured smile on her face as she said, "Call me Mom, and I will see you again, I know it."

There must be something about the women in this family...

Chapter 16

As we drove away, Mary said, "I owe you big time for this one, Mel, they really bought us as a couple, and they really liked you."

I knew that the dream would die sometime, I was just wishing that it didn't have to be so soon.

We talked the whole flight back about the weekend that was behind the two of us. Mary didn't fall asleep on my shoulder again, and the funny thing was, I found myself wishing that she would, just one more time before our little adventure was over and we arrived at home. But we talked instead, about how great it is to see people you've been away from for a while, and how great it is to have a family.

If you haven't guessed it by now (which also means you haven't been paying any attention at all), depression was starting to set in big time here. The thought of my empty little house on Mamut Road was almost more than I could stand, and the really depressing part was that the worst week of all, the one right before Christmas, was still coming up.

When I pulled my poor old truck to the curb in front of Mary's house, I shut it off and turned to look at this travel agent that I had fallen so hard, and so completely for. I had made up my mind at last. We had spent the last two days together, acting as a couple, and by her own admission, we got along great. Her family loved me, more than I could have ever hoped that they would, and I knew that Mary placed a lot of importance on her family's opinions, even if she didn't always follow their advice. I had spent the last five hundred miles convincing myself that now was the time, that everything was perfect, and that it was going to work.

The woman I loved looked across the cab at me as I turned to face her with my true feelings on the tip of my tongue, and she said to me, "Thanks for everything, Mel. I'll find a way to make this up to you."

I took a deep breath and prepared to say the most important thing in my life. Unaware, Mary continued, "I'm just really lucky to have you as a friend, and I don't want anything change that."

Oh well, so much for that idea.

Funny thing about confidence, it just doesn't stick around very long. She gave me a quick hug and promised to see me later.

As she slammed the door on the pickup, I waved back at her from the bottom of a dark pit of very cliched despair. I watched her go into the house and spent some time pounding my head against the steering wheel. Apparently, that was enough to call up both Andy and Jake, because all of the sudden they were sitting in the cab with me.

Andy almost screeched as she asked, "Why did you stop? Why didn't you tell her? It would've been perfect..."

"Should've told her, man," was all Jake had to say. Thank God.

"You guys heard what she said, she doesn't want to lose me as a friend, no matter what. I just couldn't tell her."

"Don't tell me that we're going to have to go through the whole thing about how you can still be friends even if you're having a serious relationship..."Andy let her head flop back onto the top of the seat as she said it, staring at the ceiling in disgust.

"No, Andy, that's not going to be necessary. But I guess I'm just not ready to tell her yet."

"If you're not careful," Jake said, "you might never be ready."

A thought had occurred to me when T.G. was telling me about all of her past boyfriends. It just seemed like there was a definite pattern emerging here, so I decided it was time to make another trip to the library. The little old ladies at the library were obviously still worried about my sexual orientation as the librarian asked me in polite conversation whether or not I had met a single guy that had just moved to town. Her words were something like "He's a really nice boy, and I think you two would hit it off really well."

No I hadn't met him, but was her granddaughter still stripping down at the Peacock Club on Saturday nights? I had always thought that she was such a sweetheart, even if she does take her clothes off for a living, and what a dancer she is! You must be very proud.

Needless to say, that particular blue-hair never poked her nose into my business again (except to try and set me up with her granddaughter).

It may have taken me a while to find what I was looking for if I wasn't so familiar with the psychology section of our public library, having looked into my own problems on several occasions. I knew that I was dealing with a pretty hot topic when I couldn't find too much on the subject of abusive relationships. I took that to mean that the pros were still making way too much money on the subject to start giving away information.

I still managed to find out quite a bit though. The catchword here seems to be, "co-dependency" and it has to do with getting your emotions from someone other than yourself. It didn't take me long to realize how serious this thing is to the people involved because, like all things in love, we tend to discount what we don't want to see.

Sadly though, after two days of solid deliberation, I came to the conclusion that there wasn't much I could do for Mary until she decided to fix the problem on her own. Unless I could get her to see that she deserved the best (that being me?) in her life, it would be up to her to realize that.

Being aware of this thing that causes us to choose relationships that are doomed from the first would be my first big step in helping my Goddess to help herself. After that, who knows?

That Wednesday found me in town finishing up what little

shopping I had to do, and having lunch with Mary and Susan. Neither one of us had a chance to fill Sue in on the "success" of our trip to the mountains of New Mexico, so Mary was giving her the full story. About how much fun we had acting as a couple, and how great I was and then she said, "And we were great together."

Those exact words came directly out of her mouth. I couldn't believe it.

"Did she just say what I thought she said?" Jake was as incredulous as I was.

Andy explained for the both of us, "She said it, and didn't even hear it."

Luckily for me, Mary had to leave right before I attempted to remove my own spleen with one of those big toothpicks that they give you with a club sandwich.

The bell on the restaurant's front door clanged shut behind her as the body heat from her good-bye hug seemed to concentrate in my cheeks. I looked at Sue and said, "Kill me now, please. Don't make me go through this anymore."

She just shook her head at me, almost as tired of this stalemate as I was. "Get it over with, Mel, tell her how you feel. Tell her the truth."

"I almost did when we got back from New Mexico, but she said something that stopped me. She doesn't want to lose me as a friend. It just wouldn't work, Sue, Mary still thinks of me as a good friend. Nothing more. It's more than a little twisted, but that's the truth you keep talking about."

The restaurant manager, a really nice guy named Leon (and you don't find too many nice guys named Leon these days), came out of the kitchen with a sheaf of papers in one hand and a pen in the other. He sat down beside Sue and handed the papers across to me.

"The bank wanted you to sign those papers yesterday, Boss," he said.

Sue stared at us with a funny look on her face as I said, "You know I hate doing this stuff so close to Christmas. I'm always afraid that somewhere down the road, some poor bean counter is going to have to work on Christmas Eve to finish the deal. And how many times do I have to tell you not to call me Boss?"

Leon just shrugged his shoulders at me, "But you are the boss, Boss." He does it just to irritate me.

"What the hell is going on here?" Sue was not as loud as usual, but we still got the general ideas.

"What do you mean?" I asked.

"Don't give me that, Mel." She was acting mad again. "When did you get into the restaurant business?"

Deciding that she had suffered long enough, I said, "It's been about, what, Leon?" I looked at my partner for assurance. "Six months more or less. Leon didn't want to own the place anymore, just run it. So, I bought it from him."

"Why would you do something like that?" Sue wanted to know.

"The IRS doesn't seem to like the word 'writer' on their little tax forms, but they don't seem to mind 'restauranteur' near as much. I get to keep some of my money now, instead of giving it all away. And besides, Leon does all the work..."

"For which I am very well paid," Leon interjected.

"...and all I have to do is sign papers once in a while. Besides, didn't you notice when it became Mel's Diner?"

Sue was on the defensive now, which experience has taught me is the best place for her to be. It didn't surprise me that she hadn't noticed the change of hands, because it was handled very quietly, and the only sign in the place was a placemat that Annie had written "Mel's" on and stuck it in a corner window before she took off with Mr. Wonderful for parts unknown. I don't think she ever did figure out who the new owner was. Thank God.

My pet store owner buddy obviously didn't like the sudden turn in the conversation because she immediately switched gears. "So what made you do this?"

I just shrugged again and said, "I might run out of ideas some day, you can never tell. This place makes both of us," my nod included Leon, "a little money."

"I'm just as happy with a little less money and a lot less worries,"

Leon added.

"There you have it. I am now officially in the burger business. Born the son of a sharecropper in the deep, deep south..." I finished in my best Robin Leech voice, which isn't saying much, but when the idea is to be annoying as possible, it's easy.

"Does Mary know about this?" Sue asked.

"I don't think so, why?"

"Maybe this is a way of impressing her, making her think of you as some kind of stable, upstanding kind of guy."

I laughed at that and said, "If she thought that I was any more stable, I'd have to be dead." I wasn't denying what Sue was saying, I just didn't want to agree with her. "Besides that, if you think of any way for me to impress the charming Ms. Byrd, and don't tell me about it, you're going to be in big trouble."

Hearing the door open and someone trying to stomp the three inches of new snow off of their boots, I turned to see the UPS man looking around the diner. To my surprise, when he spotted me, he headed right over to the table and gave me a small package. Jim (the UPS guy) said, "You can always tell a single guy. He'll get everything through the mail. Gifts, clothes, computer disks. I haven't had to bring you any wine lately though, Mel. What's the deal?"

"I guess I haven't needed it lately," I answered him.

He also accepted my invitation for a cup of coffee, which Leon went to get for him. Sue asked me what the package was and I just told her that she'd have to wait. We talked with Jim about the sudden approach of the holidays, and the weather, but pretty soon he said that if he ever expected to get the day over with, that he had to get going. He tried to pay for his coffee, but I managed to toss fifty cents down on the table before he could get his hand out of his pant's pocket.

Jim just looked at Sue and said, "You wouldn't think that he owns the place the way he acts, would you?"

Susan's face got red as she asked, "Am I the only one that didn't know about this?"

I smiled at her as I sat back in the booth and said, "Almost."

Walking home from the diner, I once more let my feet lead me off of my designated path to the courthouse park. Just standing there looking at that nativity scene seemed to ease the loss of family a little for me. It was a part of me that had really been hurting since the weekend with Mary's entire family. Those old holiday feelings kept coming back to me, more and more every day. Would I ever find anyone to be with, would I ever have a family of my own? Or would I die alone, bitter and unhappy in my old age? The memory of those two girls laughing at me as I walked away from them on Main Street came back to me. Would I just become the weird old guy that lives at the end of Mamut Road?

Hearing footsteps beside me brought me out of my self-pity, and I wasn't surprised to find Carl Boothby, the old groundskeeper, standing beside me, also looking at the nativity.

"You sure do spend a lot of time staring at that thing, kid." He growled at me.

"You seem to spend a lot of time talking, old man." I snarled back at him.

We slowly turned to look at each other, smiling over our private little joke as I asked, "How you doin', Booth?"

"'Bout like always, Mel," Carl said. He was a bent and tired man of about seventy-five, with a thick shock of silver hair on his head, and a pair of pliers always handy in his pocket.

He pulled off his glasses and gave them a good polishing before he asked, "You never did tell me why you like that little lamb so much, Kid. What's the deal?"

Shrugging my shoulders, I gave him the truth. "I used to get to play the lamb in the Christmas pageant when I was a kid. I guess it kind of makes me think about when things were a little simpler, and a lot happier."

"And maybe not so lonely?" he asked.

My head whipped around and I stared at the old man for a second before I asked, "What would make you think that?"

He just shrugged a hauntingly familiar shrug and said, "It's easy for me to recognize someone that's lonely. I know what it looks like."

I thought about that for a few moments in the midst of our companionable silence. I'd never thought about Carl being all alone in this world, but when I thought about it, I knew that he had no family here in town. I thought about it for a while longer before I asked, "What have you got going for Christmas Eve, Booth?"

"Same ol' thing," he replied. If I hadn't known better, I would have thought that he meant spending it with his wife and kids. At least, that's what everybody else in town thought he meant. "Why do you ask?"

"Do you know Eric and Sue Oaks?"

"Sure," he said, "nice people."

"You are officially invited to their house for Christmas Eve dinner at six-thirty on Friday."

"Are you sure that it'll be all right?" he asked.

"Don't worry, Booth," I told him as I clapped him lightly on the arm, "I'll take the heat."

The smile on his face as I walked away was more than enough thanks for me.

Chapter 17

Christmas Eve came soon enough after that, and before long, I found myself on the Oak's doorstep with a load of Christmas goodies in my arms, even some that had been hastily purchased for old Boothby, trying to ring the doorbell with my nose (I wasn't going to try it with my tongue anyway, it was below zero). Eric opened the door with eggnog on one hand and a sprig of mistletoe in the other.

I raised one eyebrow at him as he said, "Aw hell, I was hoping it was Mary." I was hoping that he hadn't drank so much eggnog that he wouldn't notice the difference, but instead he called over his shoulder, "Honey, this one's for you."

Sue came sprinting out of the kitchen and gave me a sound kiss on the cheek and ran back to her stove as I yelled to her rapidly retreating back, "Merry Christmas to you too!"

Eric laughed and said, "She's got something going in there that she doesn't want to leave for very long. Go ahead and put your loot under the tree, and I'll get you an eggnog."

I deposited the presents and spent a second or two arranging them. Eric brought me the traditional eggnog, and I asked him if I was too early.

"No such thing this time of year, Mel, you can keep me out of trouble by keeping me out of the kitchen."

"Are you guys sure it was all right to invite Boothby? I just didn't want him to be alone, especially tonight."

"No problem at all, Mel. I'll show you what Sue got him."

Following him into a back bedroom, he knelt down by a suspicious looking cardboard box. It was suspicious because its top was full of air holes. Eric opened it up and revealed a yellow lab puppy asleep in the corner. I guess I don't have to say that he was cute, all puppies are cute, but this one was really cute.

I gave it a double thumbs up.

Mary showed up and Eric finally got to give somebody a kiss. There was a brief spat over who would get to kiss Carl when he showed up, but it was finally decided that both ladies would get the honor.

We waited for the groundskeeper patiently as Sue finished getting dinner ready, and when a knock came at the door, we all assumed it was him. I went to answer it and was surprised to find the county sheriff waiting on the doorstep.

"Oh good, I was hoping you were here, Mel." He was holding a good-sized cardboard box in front of him, which he handed to me as I asked him to come in.

He sighed once the door shut behind him and said, "I've got some bad news, Mel. We found Carl Boothby this afternoon... We missed him when he didn't show up for the courthouse Christmas party. Anyway, we found him in his house, apparently he'd laid down to take a nap after lunch and never woke up."

I staggered a little and leaned against the doorframe for support, as the sheriff continued, "I didn't know that you and Carl were close, but this package for you was by his back door, all ready to go." I mumbled something about how the old man was coming here for dinner tonight as I stared at the box that I'd set on the floor.

I opened it gingerly with my shaking fingers to find the antique lamb from the nativity scene inside. There was a letter with it that I crushed in my hand as I pulled out the innocent little lamb.

I'm afraid that I don't remember much for a while after that, just that I was stumbling through the deep snow with no real idea of where I was going. When I realized where I was, I found myself kneeling in front of that stable scene again, fresh snow covering the figures and falling all around me. I reached out carefully and brushed the snow off the carved wood, figuring that Boothby wouldn't mind me taking care of them for him just this once.

Feeling someone beside me, I turned to see Mary kneeling next to me in the snow, my forgotten coat in her hands. I fought back the tears and sadness as I put the lamb back in its rightful place, and handed Mary the letter that had gone along with it, asking her to read it for me.

I watched as she smoothed the wrinkled paper and read softly aloud.

"Mel, You've been a good friend to me and I want you to have this so you can always remember that a man needs people around him. If you forget that, you lose everything. I'm proof of that. Thanks again for being my friend. Always, Boothby."

I looked at Mary with the tears freezing to my face as I said, "I don't want to die alone."

"You won't Mel." Mary was as scared as hell, and I didn't want that. "I'll always be with you." She wrapped her arms around me as she said, "I'll always be your friend."

I just held on to her with everything I had in me. I was just happy that she was there, I didn't care why. The silent snow fell all around us as the moon bathed the town square in its cool, serene light. The sounds of carolers drifted into my ears, reminding me again of how important people are to us all.

The next morning, I insisted that they all go ahead and open the presents without me, using the excuse that I didn't want to ruin their Christmas by being depressed, which was truthfully no excuse, but I needed to get away and go for a long run, trying to figure out Boothby's last message to me. I spent all of Christmas Day running on the mountain, trying to work through all of my feelings to the truth of the old man's gift.

I watched the sun set from a chunk of rock that had been cleared of snow by the mountain wind and that overlooked our entire valley. The little town of Browning only took up one tiny corner of what I could see from here. Maybe there was some symbolism in that, but it brought me no closer to what I needed to know than I had been when the day began.

Sue told me early the next morning that Mary had actually cried when she opened my gift the day before. The antique crystal ornament had come express from a New York City auction house, where Rick Jamison had finally located it for me. It had been a part of a private collection and as near as my editor and I could tell, it was the only one of its kind in the United States, besides the one on Estelle's tree. The cost of this type of ornaments had gone up considerably in the last ten years, due in part to a story told about the old man who had hand crafted the two matched ornaments. It seemed that before the old man died he had practically given one of the pair to a little girl who had written him from somewhere in New Mexico. When he passed on, the other was sold to the auction house, and I can personally vouch for the fact that they were very proud of that ornament. It had taken a lot of string pulling to get the ornament here before Christmas. Thank God for UPS, huh?

I'd only written one thing on the plain white card that I enclosed with it. "You should have everything you want in life. You deserve it."

And what did Mary have to say about it? Well, she came out to the little house on Mamut Road the day after Christmas. I answered the door with more than a little fear, unsure of how she would act towards me after the gift. Had it been too much, too corny maybe? Would she be freaked out about the way I acted when I heard about...I steeled myself against the force of the thought, when I heard about Boothby's death?

I put all those thoughts behind me when she threw her arms around my neck as I opened the door. Mary stood back and looked into my eyes (I hate it when she does that, I'm always afraid that she'll see something that I don't want her to see), and told me that she loved the ornament and it was the sweetest thing anyone had ever done for her.

When my knees quit wobbling, I took her coat and hung it in what passed for a closet around here, as she walked over to my little used fireplace. As I joined her, Mary looked over her shoulder at me with real concern in her eyes that made me feel better than I had in days.

"Are you all right?" she asked softly.

"Yeah, I am." I stuck my hands in my pants pockets and looked at my shoes, kind of silly considering everything that we'd been through together, but I really couldn't help it. "Thank you for...you know, the other night..."

"It's all right..." She tried to stop me.

"No, I want to tell you that," I was having trouble with the words, "it really meant a lot to me." It was all I could handle telling her right now.

"I told you, Mel," she said, "I'll always be your friend."

Nasty thing, the emotional punch to the breadbasket. Ask the man who gets one every day.

Mary knelt by my fireplace to look at the antique lamb in its new position of honor among the other important things in my life. My father's tiny cobbler's anvil was there along with the chest that my great-grandmother had brought from Scotland.

"What did he mean by what he said in the letter?" she wanted to know.

It was the one thing she wanted to know and I really couldn't tell her. "It was something the two of us had talked about before. Boothby and I agreed that no one should live alone. We both knew it, but we thought we were powerless to change it." But were we really powerless? Was that what he'd meant, that we all have the power to change our own lives?

I was still thinking about it when the four of us stood in respectful silence as the priest said a few quiet words over the casket they were getting ready to lower into the ground. It shocked and saddened me that we were the only ones at the services. It also scared the hell out of me as the truth in Boothby's letter finally came through to me in that cold, lonely cemetery, with only a few strangers to mark the passing of a good man.

The waitress that had gotten Annie's old job, she's a grandmother by the way, brought me a cup of coffee as I sat down in the same booth as always. The winter outside the plate glass window had slowly leveled off at just plain awful. Now that the new year had started, it would begin to lighten up until spring arrived. Of course we always had late snowstorms in the high country, but the snow never stays for long. The thought that spring was on its way scared me more than just a little. I had promised myself that I wouldn't let this one-sided love affair drag on forever, it just hurt too much to be around this beautiful woman day in and day out and not tell her how I felt about her. The opportunity came a dozen times a day, and still, I knew what her answer would be to a premature confession of my affections. I would have tried anyway, but I guess what stopped me was the fact that it would probably hurt her as much as it hurt me. She just didn't need me dumping all of this on her right now, and I could even see what the pity in her eyes would look like if I thought about it hard enough. There was always more than just pity in her eyes, there was pain too. And that was something that I just wouldn't do. Couldn't do.

I shook my head to bring myself out of my self-induced deep blue funk as the object of my secret affections slid into the seat across from me. I smiled my best smile at her as Susan sat down next to me, throwing an arm around my shoulders as she said, "What are you in such a good mood about?"

I shrugged my shoulders and said, "Just happy to be alive, and in the company of good friends."

"Smart boy, isn't he?" Mary was in a pretty good mood these days now that the Holidays from Hell were behind us.

"Very." Susan was obviously thinking to the contrary, given my present self-induced situation, and I was beginning to agree with her.

I felt Andy nudge me in a not so gentle reminder of the double purpose of today's lunch. I didn't have time to wonder about being nudged by a female mercenary type before I whipped my trusty notebook out of my shirt pocket and asked, "You guys are women, right?"

They just looked at each other for a second before Mary said, "He kind of destroyed the point I was just trying to make, didn't he?"

"Yes he did," Sue answered Mary as she turned to me, "what are you getting at?"

I stuttered my apologies as I tried to explain, "My editor wants me to try writing a different kind of book. He thinks it'll help both our careers if we put out a book on how to pick up women."

Susan wasn't much help for the next minute or two, I actually had to grab her arm to keep her from falling out of the booth. Mary simply covered her mouth with her hand during Sue's gales of laughter. I love loyalty in a woman. I love loyalty in anyone.

"A...book...women!" Susan was starting to regain her breath and her wit. She was still laughing when I shoved her out on the floor. Why did I even bother catching her?

"So, Mary," I tried to act like I was ignoring the still giggling woman climbing back onto her seat, "what do you think women want in a man?"

She didn't act really confident as Mary said, "Are you sure you want to ask me a question like that, Mel? I mean, my past record doesn't exactly make me a top candidate for the happiness crowd."

"Get real, darlin'." If she froze up on me, Andy's well laid (a figure of speech) plan would crash and burn. "We are talking about a book that will be read by lonely, desperate men in hopes of finding someone who won't mind that they're living in their parent's basement. Or even more desperate women who want to recreate themselves in the image of what I say men want. What could be sadder than that?"

Mary was slightly alarmed as she said, "How about the fact that I never thought of trying that. Is the library open today?" She had started to slide out of the booth when my head hit the table with a sound smack. Great, now both of them were laughing.

At least when they calmed down a little bit the ladies were ready to help me.

"All right, Mel," Susan said, "we'll help you as much as we can, won't we, Mary?"

"Sure," Mary answered her.

"I really think that the average woman just wants someone who..." Susan started.

"Yeah, yeah, that's nice Sue," I cut in before she could really get started, "how about you, Mary?"

She took a deep breath and thought about it for a moment before she said, "I don't really know, Mel. I guess you just know when you see him."

I shook my head at her. "There's got to be more to it than just that. I mean, I know that everyone wants something different, but there has to be something basic that you're after."

She looked puzzled for a second as she said, "I guess, but it's..." Mary stopped, and looked embarrassed.

It felt like she was right on the verge of something important, so I nudged her as gently as I could.

"Well?" Oh yeah, the real sensitive guy.

Mary just frowned at me and said, "To be truthful, there's something about a man who's a little bit dangerous, isn't there, Sue?" She looked across the booth for a little support.

"Well, I guess." Susan didn't sound so sure herself. "I kind of gave that up early on in life. It seemed like a wise move at the time, still does as a matter of fact."

"What do you mean by 'dangerous'?" I still needed a little bit more to go on.

"I really don't know how to explain it, Mel, But it's not someone who you know will be there if you need him, someone reliable, someone like..."

Me? Ouch.

It was my turn to be embarrassed as I said, "I think I understand now."

Chapter 18

Things were going great. Everything is just like we thought it was going to be. It's going to be all right. I just kept telling myself over and over. The sad thing was, that I wasn't even buying what I was selling.

Mary had left to sell a package vacation to a bunch of Moose Lodge members, so I sat there and kept trying to convince myself that I was in control of my situation. It wasn't working.

It didn't take long for Sue to speak up. "That was a pretty slick move, Mel. It's just too bad that it didn't work out any better than it did."

"Yeah, I know I didn't need to hear what she told me. Doesn't exactly make me feel like kicking up my heels." I even sounded depressed as hell.

Susan reached across the booth and ruffled my hair. "I know, Mel," she said as she got up to leave, "you go home and think about it for a while and maybe you'll come up with something you can work with."

"Are you completely blind or just dumb?" Andy started in before I could even make it all the way home.

"Not you, too?" I was in no mood for this, walking home in the snow on top of everything else.

"Mel," she was almost being contrite, "you know I love you, but sometimes you can really be thick."

I resigned myself to fate and asked, "What do you have in mind?"

Andy had a very familiar smile on her face as she said, "We'll make you into one bad boy when the time comes."

"When the time comes?" She was confusing me again and I hate that.

"I should have you ready by springtime." Andy sounded confident.

"That's a long time to wait." I wasn't sure that I could stand the current situation for that long.

"We've got a lot of work to do," she answered.

"You want something to drive that just screams Rebel!" Jake was sure about this, as we discussed their plan later in the day.

"But I'm not a rebel, Jake. I'm a long way from it as a matter of fact. And what good would it do me anyway?" I was pretty sure myself on this subject.

"I'll prove it to you," he said, a smug smile on his face that looked kind of familiar. "Watch this..."

A huge motorcycle appeared in my living room as if by magic. Chrome and black paint dominated the huge, fat fenders and the tiny puddle of oil beneath it. I looked to Jake for an explanation, or at least one hell of a story.

"If you play around in somebody's mind long enough, you learn a few tricks."

I watched in fascination as M.P.H. called to his counterpart in the kitchen where she was devouring the last of my fat-free yogurt (no great loss). Andy entered the room and her face lit up like a kid's on Christmas morning. She ran to the bike, saying, "Great bike! Who's going to take me for a ride..."

Andy threw a leg over the seat but when she tried to sit down, I watched in amazement as she fell through the bike, landing her attractive butt on the floor with a solid thump. "A hallucination." I was starting to understand as I watched the bike disappear, leaving Andy sitting in the middle of the floor all by herself. "It was a hallucination."

"Right," Jake said, "and because Andy is a part of you, she saw it too."

I walked over and gave Andy a gentlemanly hand to her feet. Jake (being Jake) offered to kiss her booboo and make it better. She turned him down with an unkind remark and gave me a kiss on the cheek, remarking that it's nice that some men can still be chivalrous. It must be true, for both Jake and I that a man can't change even if he wants to. At least, that's what I was thinking when I gave Jake my own "I hope you're jealous" look. I guess that must be the basic difference between the two of us. Jake and I, he couldn't be a gentleman if he wanted to, and I couldn't be anything else. I brought up the fact that I really didn't think that I would be able to change who I was in an effort to win Mary over.

"We're not going to change you forever, Mel. It's just going to be on the surface, you can do this," Jake said. I still wasn't too sure about it, so Jake continued in an attempt to change the subject, back to one he had control of.

"The point being, Mel," Jake was pointing wildly at Andy, "that a bike is a definite babe magnet. They just can't help it."

"True enough." Andy was still rubbing her sore spots, agreeing with Jake despite the trick he'd just pulled on her to prove a point. "Obviously."

"So where do we find this sure fire babe getter?" I wanted to know.

I should've known that he'd show me.

Both Jake and Andy now sat on either side of me as I cranked out yet another round of setups. With a common goal in mind the two of them made quite an imposing force. They were trying to recreate me in their image. Andy was right, they had a lot of work to do.

"The important thing is," Jake was saying, "that she doesn't see any change in the man that she has lunch with all the time."

"True," Andy agreed with him, "but I don't think that's going to be so hard. She won't see any change in Mel because she won't let herself see it."

"Hold it a second you two," I interrupted them, "what kind of changes are we talking about here?"

"You heard what she said, Mel." Jake threw me a towel as I finished my setups. "She is drawn to a man that is dangerous. Someone that it's a risk to love."

"Definitely not me is what you're saying." It still bothered me that she wanted this kind of guy.

"No," Andy said, "not you right now. Remember, Mel, we've got all the time in the world to turn you into something that she wants."

I still wasn't sure as I said, "What good will it do to change me for her? I shouldn't have to overhaul my entire psyche just to make her notice me."

"We're not talking about anything permanent here, Mel, are we, Andy?" Jake was being supportive again, and that still makes me nervous.

"No, of course not," she answered. "We just have to change the way that she sees you, and that's going to take some major shock power." I could see an idea growing in her eyes. "It's almost as if you need to be a completely different person..."

"That's it!" Jake made us both jump. "We'll have to change him so much that she won't recognize him!"

"Whoa, whoa, whoa," I tried to stop him, "I'm not getting any plastic surgery done or anything..."

Jake just sort of frowned at me as he said, "I'm talking about attitude, Mel, but we will have to change your appearance a little, but not much."

"Attitude?"

"Yes, attitude." Jake was on a roll now. "She's got you right where she wants you now. Mary knows that you'll always be there when she needs you. You are her backup in case she needs a shoulder to cry on. Do you understand what I'm telling you?"

I thought about it for quite a while before I said, "She wouldn't do that. Not to me, not to anybody."

Andy stepped in. "Mary probably doesn't even know that she's doing it. It just happens."

Finally, I had to accept what these two were saying, even if I didn't like it. It had happened to me before, girls that just strung you along because they knew they could. Once they stopped dressing up for dates, stopped making an effort to spend time with you, you were pretty well had in the romance department. You might be the first one she'll call if she needs help moving her furniture, but that's about it. I just had to accept that Mary was a human being, not the kind of Goddess that I'd made her out to be in my own twisted mind. The Mary I wanted was the real one anyway, not my idea of who she is.

It was hard work that lay ahead of the three of us. Jake and Andy would have to work with me almost day and night to pull this one off. The changes they were talking about would take a lot of concentration on my part, and that's something I've never had too much of. Creating a new personality for me would not be easy, especially since it would have to be so different from the way I really am.

"You can do this, Mel." Andy always seemed optimistic, a strange balance to Jake's constant pessimism. "You're smart enough to pull this off, and you've already created two of us with your screwed up head, this should be easy for you."

I still wasn't real sure about this whole thing. "Yeah right, just a walk in the park of my sub-conscious mind."

She just smiled at me and said, "Time for another trip to the library."

Browsing through the local library had been one of my favorite past-times for a long time, but I'd never found myself in this particular section before. Several women were sitting around reading, looking for the perfect escape from our less than perfect world, or maybe they wanted something to do so they wouldn't have to talk to their husbands for a while. Whatever the reason for them being here, they were sure that I didn't belong. I cleared my throat quietly, nodded to the ladies that were giving me the worst stares, and quickly thumbed through the section that I lovingly refer to as "Heaving Bosom Fiction." Grabbing as many books as I could without attracting jealous stares, I made a break for the neutral territory by the magazine racks. Sitting down at my usual table, I started looking through my recently acquired bounty.

As I walked to the librarian's desk, I passed the reference section. A book that I'd looked at often before jumped off the shelf at me. When I first started seeing Jake, I'd rushed to the library and found this book. Reaching out and plucking it off the shelf felt like saying hello to an old friend (I never said I had a real life). *Psychological Manifestations* by the respected Dr. Niles Crane had led me to the inescapable conclusion that I should seek competent professional help. Unfortunately, the closest thing to a psychiatrist in this town would have to be the bartender at the Broken Spur, and I was pretty sure that he'd just tell me that I was crazy, and that I should drink more.

While Dr. Crane's ramblings didn't help me to cure my problem, it did help me figure out what it was. Little kids have imaginary friends all the time, and Niles was sure that this would cause no hardship to the tikes later on in their lives, so I could only hope the same would hold true for me.

The truth of the matter was that this new idea of the Terrible Twos scared me because I wasn't sure if my poor, battered psyche could take it. I slipped the book onto the pile that I was getting ready to check out and made my way carefully to the desk.

When I got home with my "research material," Andy was waiting for me, anxious to find out where we were headed. Of course, she reached right out the very first thing and snagged the pre-eminent Dr. Crane right off the top of the stack. She looked at me very carefully as she finished reading the dustcover.

"What is it, Mel?" she asked, "Don't you trust us?"

I didn't mean to, honest I didn't, but I laughed out loud. "How can I trust you two? Jake has never done anything but get me into more trouble than I could handle, and you haven't been around enough for me to even start trusting you. I'm just afraid that nobody out there gives a damn whether or not I'm...I'm..."

"Crazy?" Her voice was soft as I sagged to my easy chair. I looked at her, the anger fading quickly from my eyes as I nodded my head.

She reached out and ruffled my hair, just like Mary had done that day in the café, and said, "You know what they say, Mel, if you can still ask 'Am I crazy?' then you're probably not."

Smiling back at her, I said, "Thanks, I'll just have to remember to keep asking that question."

Chapter 19

The next few months had to be the longest of my life. Andy and Jake worked with me night and day, just as I was afraid they would. The romance novels were followed by all the books on acting that our local library had. I had to learn how to separate this "dangerous guy" that the Terrible Two wanted me to be from the "harmless guy" that I really am. Good actors, so they say, can slip in and out of character when somebody yells action. That was what I had to do. Can you see why I was afraid I might go off the deep end?

What about the romance novels you ask? They held an unbelievable amount of information. It was easy to see why women are so disappointed with the men in their lives. When they hit page number 479, the often imperiled heroine finally gets the Prince Charming of this perfect little world, and she closes the book to find...well, no Prince Charming.

The main plot line that I could find among these pearls of literary beauty seemed to be that the ladies (some of whom were no ladies) never believed that they would get to spend the rest of their lives with the guy they exchanged smoldering glances with throughout the entire book. He was always unattainable. Maybe that old tale about wanting something that you can't have works on women, too. It must be kind of like what happens the minute the average man gets a girlfriend. Women come out of the woodwork to hit on the poor guy once they realize he can't be had. Maybe they've got some kind of radar that tells them that another woman has him, and it drives them crazy.

And the men of the romance world? These bad boy bodice rippers always say the right thing in order to talk the poor innocent girl (if you read Danielle Steel) into something she'll certainly regret in the morning. But, if you read Jackie Collins, it's usually the other way around, with the ladies doing their fair share of the seducing (and watch out for the buttons on your silk shirt). He's always well muscled, tanned and usually rich. He has the ability to catch her attention by conspicuously sleeping around, or by ignoring her all together. He has the pick-up lines that she loves to hear, like, "how 'bout a backrub?' or maybe "c'mere." Like that works in real life. Successful businesswomen reduced to a pile of goo by "c'mere"? It must be in the build-up. I hope.

She sees him across the crowded room at the opening of her new branch office, or the unveiling of his latest sculpture. They exchange those lusty glances through the first hundred pages, or until he catches her skinny-dipping in the local, secluded pond. Oh yeah, that happens. Or maybe she watches him drink a Diet Coke when he's working construction...

I could tell already that the build up was going to be the hard part, and the most important.

I even managed to stop feeling guilty about not writing enough by actually spending some time at the word-processor. Andy was with me the whole way on this "How To" book that Jamison had me doing, helping me to put my thoughts on the subject down in a somewhat solid form. Not that I believed for one second that any of the advice I was giving in this book would help some poor shmuck get himself a new cave-partner, but as long as I was going to do it, I would do my best to make it work. Having Andy around to act as a sounding board for my befuddled ideas on the state of womanhood was proving to be beneficial. The more I talked to The Lady Mercenary, the more I learned, even if, technically speaking, I was just rehashing things that I already knew in some part of my mind.

Remember when I said that Jake would show me where to find a motorcycle? Well, somewhere in my past, I had seen an old motorcycle waiting patiently to be restored to its former glory, and Jake remembered where it was.

Leon and I stood in the old garage behind his house looking at the disaster before us. It would've been nice if all the old bike had needed was a fresh coat of paint and an oil change, but I've never done anything the easy way before in my life, so why start now? It lay in several pieces with the tires rotting off of the rims and the motor lying in the dirt and the dust, collecting its share of rust and spiders.

"I've been gonna restore her for years..." Leon said, sounding almost sad, "but I realize now that I'm never gonna have the time to do it, what with the grandkids and all."

I kneeled down among the pieces and asked, "Is she all here?"

"Oh yeah," Leon said. "I've even got the original owners manual and several books about it that I've bought over the years. Lots of articles from motorcycle magazines and such."

"That's great," I said, a little relieved, "I'm gonna need all the help that I can get on this."

"I'd be glad to help you with it," Leon jumped in, "it'd be kind of nice to see her get all put back together."

I shook his hand to close the deal and said, "You might be sorry you ever offered."

Getting lights and heat put into my little garage at home turned out to be harder than buying something that needed a garage. The little building had been completed back when horse carriages were still in use so I had never been able to stuff my Ford into it, but it would make a nice place to work on the bike. All the electricians seemed to want to talk about was "code" this and "fire marshal" that, but eventually they got the job done.

I walked into the only car dealership in town and looked for a familiar pair of boots sticking out from under one of the cars in the service bays. I found them underneath a Volvo at the far end of the shop.

"What do you have to do to get a car fixed around here?" I asked the thin air around me.

Eric slid out from under the Volvo and answered me with, "We don't fix cars here, we just sell new ones."

"Yeah," I said, waving at the packed shop, Eric being the number one, and only, mechanic, "it doesn't look like you're busy or anything."

He wiped his hands on a grease rag and let me help him up off of the creeper. "What's going on, Mel?"

"Not much, I just need a little mechanical information."

"Ask away," he said.

"What would you torque the head bolts to on a '75 Harley Dynaglyde?"

He eyed me carefully and said, "About twenty-five pounds, and why did you go and buy Leon's bike?"

I was impressed, both the husband and the wife were sharp. That usually doesn't happen. You can figure out how it usually goes. If not, ask your wife to explain it to you.

"I don't know. I guess I want to walk on the wild side, feel the wind in my hair, the highway rumbling under me. I want to..."

"Spend six months in a body cast?" he added.

"Pretty much. Listen, Eric." I was almost pleading, but not quite. "You've ridden motorcycles all your life, you know what it's like. How can you deny me that chance?"

He thought about it for a while before saying, "You're right. If you drive like you've got a head on your shoulders, bikes aren't any more dangerous than cars, and the thrill is worth it." He smiled suddenly, "And the women. Wow."

I actually saw the light bulb go on over his head.

"So you'll help me?" I asked.

He was still smiling as he said, "Help you what? Fix up that bike? Sure I will. Who am I to deny a man his chance at the..." he paused for effect, "open road. Not to mention that I always wanted to restore something with unlimited fundage."

That made me more than a little nervous, but the deal was already made.

By the time that Eric, Leon and I had finished hauling the pieces and parts of my new motorcycle into my tiny garage, I was beginning to wonder about the intelligence of what I'd done. It lay strewn about the cement floor, looking for all the world like some fantastically difficult jig saw puzzle.

Looking at my two mechanics, I asked, "Well, what do you guys think?"

Eric took the lead and said, "I guess we'd better get started on this project. What have you got for tools, Mel?"

I gave him my patented, and very familiar, blank look and repeated, "Tools?" Did they expect me to think of everything?

Eric, having already reached the status of "disgruntled mechanic," just shook his head at me and said, "Why don't you go get my toolbox out of the back of my pickup, Mel, while Leon and I get started sorting this out."

I was the wind.

When I returned with a small metal box that was threatening to lengthen my arms by a good six inches, Eric and Leon were arguing over whether or not this part was the correct one or not, or if that part needed to be refurbished before it could be used.

I put down the box and sat on an old milk crate to study the owner's manual for a while. When I finished with that, I looked up to find the two mechanics still arguing, so I picked up a magazine to read. When I finished with the entire stack some three hours later, Eric and Leon were still arguing, but at least they had changed the subject to how to find out if the frame was bent. I fished through the stack of magazines for a few seconds, and finding the one I was looking for, walked up to the two men and handed it to them. I had even turned the page to the article on how to check motorcycle frames for damage.   The two of them stood and stared at me in silence as I walked back over to the toolbox that I had carried in, and retrieving a tape measure, threw it across the shop to them. Then I picked up a socket wrench and a few sockets and started to disassemble the motorcycle's engine.

"Whatya doin', Mel?" I heard from behind me.

"Well," I grunted an answer as I broke loose a head bolt, "I figured that we'd better get this thing apart so we could see what we need to get fixed. You know, whether the block needs honed or bored, how much work needs to be done on the heads, if the carbs are full of varnish or not, just the general stuff. How are you guys coming with the frame?"

"Oh fine, fine..." both of them said as I heard the sounds of a tape measure being used behind me. At least they'd quit arguing. Did I ever mention that I'm a quick learner about anything except women?

What the other guys couldn't see was Jake standing over my shoulder, giving me directions on exactly what it was I was doing. Apparently, everything that I'd read in the manual and magazines had been absorbed into his part of the brain, so he knew what needed to be done even if I didn't.

By the time we wrapped it up that night, we had a pretty good idea as to what we needed in the way of parts, and repairs to the engine and the rest of the bike. Both of the guys had been sworn to secrecy about our project, and Eric took off with the parts in the back of his pickup that would need to be dropped off at the machine shop, and he promised that he would leave a list at the local parts store telling me what I would need in the way of tools. Leon headed for home to grab some sleep before opening the diner the next morning.

And me? I worked on Rick's *How to Pick up Women* book for a few hours. All the stuff about women that aren't really in touch with their feelings and how they will treat you if you let them get away with it, came out in about forty pages of me being as angry as hell. The bad thing was that I really wasn't as mad at Mary or women in general as I might have let on. I was really mad at myself for not having guts enough to change my situation. Andy pointed this out to me after helping me write the last few chapters in what I'd began to call *The Book of Love.*

"I understand that you have to write this book, Mel," Andy said as I turned the processor off, "but you shouldn't use it as an excuse not to get on with your own life."

"That's not my excuse, Andy, my excuse is that I just don't have the cajones to tell Mary that I love her." I couldn't see a reason to hide the truth from myself.

"Why can't you?" she wanted to know.

I couldn't tell her that it just felt like if I tried, it wouldn't work. I have to trust my feelings here and I don't think that she can take me seriously yet. We need something else. I know it.

The next few months saw one hell of a change in that man-sized jigsaw puzzle lying on my garage floor too. My normally cluttered house became a real mess littered with every motorcycle magazine and book I could find at the library. That little old librarian was one confused lady by this stage in the game, I was considering looking into deep-sea fishing after this whole thing is over...

The poor UPS guy was now hauling huge, heavy boxes to my front door instead of the manageable ones he had gotten used to. It didn't take me long to realize that there just isn't a much prettier sight than new chrome against mile-deep black lacquer paint as I rubbed out the last coat of Eric's class one paint job. I could actually see myself in the finish as I straightened my aching back and looked out the garage door at the signs of a fast approaching spring in the mountains. The sky was that deep blue that you just don't see anywhere else (at least not anywhere that I've been) and the birds were starting to sing again.

I walked out to the driveway and was just looking at the scenery as Eric and Leon came up Mamut Road in Eric's pick-up and stopped beside me.

"What's up, Mel?" Eric asked as the truck skidded to a stop.

"Not much." I coughed as dust from the pick-up's tires engulfed me completely. "How 'bout you guys?"

I heard the doors slam shut on the truck but couldn't for the life of me actually see the two of them get out of the pickup through the dust.

"We've got your new tires." Leon's voice came out of the dust-filled air as the sun started to show through. He and Eric grabbed the tires and rims out of the box of the truck, and walked into the garage with them. I heard Eric's appreciative whistle as he inspected the finish on the bike. He was admiring his own reflection in the gas tank when I walked in and asked if my polishing met with his approval.

I grabbed some tools and started to put the wheels back on my babe-magnet as Eric said, "It's beautiful, Mel."

"It's all ready to go when those wheels are on, ain't it, Mel?" Leon asked.

"Should be..." I answered with a grunt as the socket slipped and I bashed my knuckles for the five-hundredth time since I'd started this project.

"You gonna take it into town?" Eric wanted to know.

Sensing a trap, I decided that being outnumbered, attack was a better option. "What are you guys getting at, exactly?"

They kind of looked at each other for a few seconds, passing the responsibility back and forth before Eric finally said, "Why are we keeping this a secret, Mel? I mean, most people who want a bike like this want to be seen on it, not just leave it in the garage."

I just smiled to myself (which was not easy since I was still sucking on my wounded knuckles) and said, "I can't believe that you guys waited so long to ask, but I guess all I can tell you right now is you'll find out eventually. You're just going to have to be patient."

Eric just hung his head and said, "I just knew you were gonna say something like that."

It only took us a few minutes to get the tires put on the Harley, and before I knew it, I was sitting on top of the monstrosity that I helped build, with one hand on the throttle and the other already clutching the brake. If that's not a platitude for my whole life, I don't know what is. The monster coughed to life with a rumble that was uncharacteristic even for a killer hog. Eric and Leon argued over the sound of the motor and tweaked the carbs until the bike settled into a steady lope.

Eric stood up and slapped me on the back and waved at the open garage door. My plan was to just take the big bike for a slow spin around the lawn, but when I cracked the throttle open (just a little bit, I thought) Murphy's Law reared its ugly head. If you haven't figured it out yet, the throttle stuck.

The Harley roared out of the garage with me barely clinging to its back, hellbent on destroying us both. I had a wild image in the rearview mirror for just a little more than an instant, of Eric and Leon running behind me waving their hands in the air. Like that was going to help me stop this fast lane trip to Hell. Then, over the rush of wind sailing past my ears, I heard Eric's and Leon's voices rise in unison, saying something that sounded like, "Tree! Tree!"

It took me just a couple of seconds to realize why those tough looking bikers wear those weird looking goggles because without them, you can't see. It took the wind that was generated by my rate of speed about two seconds to completely dry out my eyes, not to mention the fact that I was sure that I looked like I'd been riding the G-Force test at NASA for the last twenty-four hours. But when I did finally manage to blink, I saw (with no little pucker factor) that I was headed straight for the only pine tree within striking distance. I jerked the handle bars to the right, skidding and almost laying the big bike down on its side, but at the last second the thought entered my mind that no matter what, I wasn't going to rub out another paint job. That frantic thought gave me the strength to keep that hog on its new tires, and point it in a somewhat safe direction.

Before I even had a chance to wonder about how wonderful a thing desperation is, I was halfway down the road to town and gaining speed fast. The big kahuna god of motorcycles must have been smiling down on me right then, because he sent a squirrel to run out in front of me on the road. Why would the demise of an innocent squirrel be a good thing, you ask? Well, try as I might, I just couldn't bring myself to run over that squirrel. When I whipped the handlebars to the left, directly toward the canyon that ran beside Mamut Road, the bind in the throttle cable came out and the bike rolled to a nice gentle stop. It was gentle considering the fact that I was doing a nine-brake in order to keep from becoming some kind of ornament in the trees about a hundred feet below me.

Eric and Leon came running up beside me as I sat there in stunned silence.

I wasn't really surprised to hear them laughing, but when I turned to look at them, they were pointing at my face as they nearly rolled on that gravel road. I looked in the rearview mirror, expecting to see a small animal of some kind in my teeth, but instead all I saw was a giant, ecstatic, never-wipe-it-off-your-face grin.

I was hooked.

Looking out the front window of the aptly named Mel's Diner, I was glad to see that spring had finally come. The trees wouldn't lose the buds they'd grown to frost, and the summer animals had come back for their brief stay in the mountains. No more planning, training, or studying for what was about to happen. I was ready.

Eric sat down across from me and asked what the special was tonight, so I told him about the wonderful things that the cook could do with a breaded pork cutlet and mashed potatoes.

He just laughed and said, "You do spend way too much time in here."

"They still don't know anything about the bike, do they?" I had to ask, they being the women in our lives.

"No, they don't. Not yet anyway, and when are you going to spring it on Mary?"

"Not yet, not quite yet," I answered as mysteriously as I could.

"Sue stopped off to pick up our fourth wheel at the travel agency, so they should be here any second," Eric told me as he looked over the scanty menu.

"Is Mary bringing my stuff with her?" I was anxious to get this thing rolling.

"What stuff?"

Taking that to mean that Eric didn't know if she was or not, I answered, "She's supposed to be putting together a vacation package for me."

"Oh yeah?" Eric was always interested in the concept of vacations, as he never gets to take one. "Where are you going?"

"I won't know until she gets here, will I?" I asked him sarcastically.

It was Eric's turn to give me a funny look as he said, "You don't think I get enough of that kind of thing from my wife?"

"Sorry, guy," I said, "I'm just a little edgy today."

"Yeah right," he had to get back at me a little, "a real tough day of typing."

Laughing, I told him, "I did manage to give myself a nasty paper cut, if that counts at all."

Eric just laughed too. Before I knew what was coming up next he'd sprung a Susan trap on me. "So, what's the next plan of attack as far as Mary is concerned?"

"Whoa, who says I'm planning anything?" I gave him my best innocent look.

"My wife says, that's who." He grinned at me. "She knows that you're up to something, she just doesn't know what yet."

"So she sends you in to find out what's going on?" I was really going out on an intellectual limb.

"Yep, and you know me, I always figure that the honest approach is best." At least he was up front about it.

"I'm going to take a vacation, that's all. And I'll tell your wife that when she gets here."

"Tell me what?" Sue scared the hell out of me as she and Mary walked up and sat down in the booth, Mary throwing a friendly arm across my shoulders. I smiled at her casually, but my head felt like it was going to explode at any moment. Her touch did things to me that I never thought possible, and it was getting worse with every day that went by.

"Tell you that," I managed to answer Susan's question somehow, "I'm ready to go on a nice long vacation, if my wonderful travel agent has figured out where I'm going yet."

Mary smiled back at me and leaned in close, so she could reach into her back jean pocket. I was still thinking about how her hair smelled (and would be for the next couple of weeks) when she handed me a computer printout of my vacation itinerary.

Reading it was almost as good as actually being there as far as I was concerned, but it was easy to tell that T.G. had put a lot of work into this little jaunt.

"Well," Sue was being impatient (go figure), "where is she sending you?"

I read the list out loud, "Egypt, Spain, France, England, Ireland, then home again."

"I left all the dates as open as I could like you wanted. That way, if you want to spend some extra time in one place or another, you can."

Susan snatched the paper out of my hands and held it so she and Eric could read it.

"Three months?" Eric asked. "Do you think you can stand that long away from home?"

"I hope so, I should be back by the Fourth of July." I sounded confident because I knew where I was really going to be.

Hearing Mary sigh beside me, I turned to see she had a kind of wistful look on her face. I prodded her knee with mine and asked what was the matter.

"It's just that..." She almost looked sad. "They say that Paris is so beautiful in the spring. I guess I just wish I was going with you."

I could hear Andy in the background yelling "No, No, No!" even as I said, "Then why don't you come along?"

A big risk I know, but I knew that I could make a joke out of it if I didn't get the right response. I watched Mary very carefully as she turned to look at me, our eyes meeting for a split second before mine fell, along with my heart.

"I mean, can't you just see the two of us in the most romantic city in the world, crying to each other about how we'll never find anyone? Boohoo this, and boohoo that. The entire French population would be convinced that all Americans are either crazy or stupid."

Bless her heart, she came up game. "You being the stupid one of course."

"What else?"

I heard Susan start to breathe again, and found myself wondering how long ago she'd stopped.

170

Chapter 20

Having said all of my good-byes, I was finally ready to put Jake and Andy's plan into action.

"Did you call all of the places on your itinerary to cancel your reservations?" Andy wanted to know.

"Yes, I did." I didn't even want to think about the implications of a sexy mercenary with maternal instincts.

"Did you pack everything that you're going to need?"

"I hope so." I was being really patient, relieved to be getting this thing under way.

"Did you..."

"Yes, I packed my toothbrush and my jammies. Can we get this show on the road?"

Andy just gave me the classic hands on hips frown and said, "All right, wise guy, get the hell out of here."

An hour later found me checked into a motel in the city, with a bankroll in my pocket and several weeks to spend a good chunk of it. The plan was to do some severe cosmetic changes over the next couple of weeks, the important changes to my poor mind having already been done. First thing was to start working on my non-existent tan. I walked down the block to a place that had a doubtful looking sign in the window that screamed out "Tanning Beds." Before long, I'd signed up for more sessions in the next two weeks than they usually allowed in a month. Of course, I also politely turned down a young lady's offer for a hundred dollar back rub, so I got the idea that no one was going to turn me into the cancer police for over tanning.

I spent the rest of my time locked up in my tiny motel room, going over my new persona, giving it a few final touches here and there. Finally, I would swear that my body would glow in the dark, but I'd acquired a nice even, store-bought suntan.

Next up was a trip further on down the block to a beauty shop called "The Bower of Pulchritude." I never would have believed that the place could stand up to the name, but it did. Inside, I found Mabel. She'd been a hairdresser in this same shop through the last thirty years and some ten odd name changes. "You want me to do what?" She didn't even remove the generic cigarette from between her lips as she said it.

"I want you to make me look tough, you know, mean. Like a biker or something. Rugged, kind of." I was trying to be precise.

Mabel just looked at me and said, "Oh. Why didn't you just say so in the first place?"

She sat up the chair when she finished, gave it a playful spin and asked, "Is that tough enough for you?"

I slowly opened my eyes and took a long look at myself. She had bleached my dark brown hair and recent growth of beard past blonde into white. Then she cut it short. I mean really short. I even had those little spikes on top of my head.

"It's perfect, Mabel. Just perfect."

She sold me enough bleach for the next two months and some gel of some kind for my beard, telling me to watch it closely for the roots to start showing.

I told her thanks, but when I started to walk out the door, she yelled, "Are you sure you didn't rob a bank or something?"

I smiled back at her and used a little bit of the new me, "No, but I'm out to steal some hearts."

It took me a while but I finally found an optometrist that didn't pull double duty as a tattoo specialist. It also took me a while to get used to the contacts that they sold me, but they made me look...well, they made me look like someone else. My dull brown eyes turned to ice blue as I blinked away saline solution and faced the almost new me in the mirror. Close, but not quite.

The Harley Davidson Store had been expecting me for months now, maybe waiting to ambush me would be more accurate. The guy that came out to help me was one hundred percent biker with the leather vest, long hair, earring, and tattoos (done by a local eye-doctor).

"How can I help you, Buddy?" he wanted to know.

I walked out of there with a whole new wardrobe, most of which squeaked as I moved. Biker Bob had promised that he would have somebody deliver the rest of my clothes to my motel, and wished me luck as he counted the roll of bills I'd just given him. I was sure that he would have a good time in Aruba, so I told him thanks and exited stage left.

I stood in front of the mirror in my motel room and studied what I saw. Andy and Jake stood behind me, doing the same thing. The old leather coat smelled like gun oil, which made me more than a little nervous about its former owner, but it was mine now. The chaps were worn too, where they had rubbed against the gas tank of an old hog for a lot of miles. Worn out jeans and a T-shirt from a bar in Mexico helped with the image that was topped off by tanker boots that had seen better days. I even had a wallet on a chain. Cool, huh?

"It's a little late to say anything now if you're not happy with the new me," I told them.

Jake just slapped me on the back and said, "You look like my kind of guy, Mel, I didn't know you had it in you."

I looked at Andy and actually caught her licking her lips like I was some kind of entree.

"Andy!" I tried to derail her train of thought.

"Huh? Oh yeah, you look okay, Mel, if you like that sort of guy." She suddenly got very interested in the color and texture of the shag carpet. I could have sworn she was blushing, but...

Jake was laughing behind me as he said, "I guess that's better proof than anything, huh, Mel?"

"Now for a real field test," I said.

I just kept repeating to myself, "attitude, attitude, and more attitude" as I rounded the corner and pulled up into the neon lit parking lot of a bar that was using the name "Sports." A couple of fellow devotees of American Iron were standing next to their own Harleys, and I decided to take a chance. Pulling right up next to them, I pushed my hog onto its kickstand, and said, "Sweet bikes."

I had two new friends.

Moose (no kidding) stood about six-five and probably weighed around two-fifty. He had arms as big as my legs, a scar on his left cheekbone where a drunk had hit him with a broken beer bottle, and wouldn't mind watching my bike for me if I wanted to go inside and try to pick up a woman.

Tony, on the other hand, was probably somewhere around five-six, and might have weighed three hundred. He'd been to the Sturgis motorcycle rally for the last twenty years running, and also wouldn't let anybody mess with my ride while I was inside.

I was ready. My new persona was wrapped around me like a blanket as I pushed my way through the door, stepping into the dark, smoky bar, letting the eardrum splitting music wash over me. I walked over to the bar slowly, deliberately letting my eyes hit every woman in the place. For the first time in my life, they were looking back at me.

So maybe these weren't the kind of women I was after, but I needed to know if they would take me seriously. I barely had time to sip my beer before I felt a tap on my shoulder. I turned, again real slow, and looked at the woman standing beside me. She was darn cute! Take away the leather and heavy makeup and you'd have...well okay, you'd have a biker chick without makeup and leather, but not too bad for my first try, and I hadn't even opened my mouth yet. Maybe that was when I'd blow it.

"What's your name, gorgeous?" Ooo, she was original too.

Now, the three of us had spent a lot of time on the proper name for the new, and supposedly improved, me. Spent a lot of time standing around arguing about it until I'd picked up the phone book and picked out my new name. Davin Rowan. Honest, I picked it right out of the book. I almost called the guy to see if women liked his name or not, but I decided to take a chance.

I did my best to snarl, and didn't do too bad. "Why, you a cop?" Her eyes got huge as she actually leaned towards me and grabbed my leather-clad arm.

"Are you," she looked around the bar suspiciously, as she popped her gum, "wanted or somethin'?"

I smiled my greasiest smile as I slid an arm around her shoulders and pulled her in next to me. "You never know in my line of work."

Now, in my own defense, I did not take this girl back to the motel with me that night. I didn't break her heart either. After I had told her all about Davin Rowan's career as a hit man for the Jamaican drug cartels (which she bought, hook, line, and sinker), I simply acted as if I recognized someone who was out to kill me, told her that I cared about her too much to put her in danger, and walked out of the place. I told the guys thanks for watching my ride and drove back to the motel. An idea was starting to form in the back of my battered skull, an idea that would either come off like gangbusters or land me in more trouble than I could stand. It was the kind of idea I was getting used to.

I needed more stuff to pull it off. Standing in front of the counter of Dob's Gun Store, I felt a little like a kid in a candy store. Dob himself was more than helpful.

"You ever bought a gun before, son?"

I jumped a little until I remembered that I had ditched the leathers and the attitude so that I wouldn't have too much trouble buying the kind of weapon that a hit man would carry.

"No sir." I tried not to put too much Beaver Cleaver into my voice. "I never have."

"Well then." He reached under the counter and brought out a Ruger SP101, and handed it to me. "How 'bout something like this?" I opened the gate on the .38 Special and looked at the cylinder politely before I handed it back to him.

"How about that Sig Sauer P229?" I just said I'd never bought one before, I didn't say I don't know anything about them.

"The SIG .357? Not too many people know about them." He looked at me for a second before he asked, "Didn't you say you'd never bought a gun before?"

"That's what I said," I answered as I popped the clip on the Sig and locked the slide back. "Do you have a Galco shoulder holster that'll fit it?"

"I can have one here for it before the waiting period is up. That'll be on the 14th." He still didn't look too sure.

"I'll see you then." I reached down on my way out and snagged one of Dob's fliers for something to read later.

"I told you all that research would come in handy someday, didn't I, Mel?" Jake was pretty proud of himself when I got back to the motel room.

"You were right, buddy, all those hours of reading *Guns & Ammo* for the Axeman series finally paid off."

I laid down next to Andy on the worn out double bed and spread the flier from Dob's out in front of us. She was still looking at me with that kind of dreamy haze in her eyes, and I was hoping to have the same effect on the charming Ms. Byrd. I leafed through the newsprint pages for a few seconds before Andy and I both saw an item at the same time. I could see the beginnings of a devious thought in the back of her mind, and I could tell it was a good one, because I was thinking the same thing.

Chapter 21

I craned my neck to look for Mary from my flat on my back position on her lobby carpet, lying in a puddle of broken glass. My first few words to her would be the most important, since if she was going to recognize my voice, she would do it right away.

"Lady," the words came out of my throat in a rasp, "you okay?"

Right away, she got mad at me. I didn't think she was being very fair since I had supposedly just saved her from rabid bikers.

"Who the hell are you? Who the hell were they and why were they trying to kill you? And me?"

For my standard tough guy answer I said nothing, just reholstering the still smoking SIG in my right hand and groaning as I attempted to stand.

Mary saw the two bullet holes that I had put in my jacket while it was draped over a fence on a country road between here and Great Falls and started to pick up the phone, wanting to call the police or an ambulance.

"No!" I gave her an urgent look, "No cops, lady, they'll be here quick enough as it is."

"But you'll die..." just like a movie heroine, only with a touch of "you idiot" thrown in for effect.

I kind of gave one of those low chuckles as I opened my Goodwill denim shirt to show her the body-armor that lay beneath it, body-armor purchased at one Dob's Gun Store.

Mary helped me into the back of the store, hiding my bike for me as police sirens wailed closer and closer. I told her then that I didn't want to put her in more danger, that she didn't need to help me any more. She told me that she had to.

Needless to say, it was a long trip to Mary's house for me after the cops left, squashed down into what she optimistically called the back seat of her Toyota. I wasn't sure if I would ever get my legs straightened again, but I was sure of the fact that if I really had cracked a rib like I told her I had, I would've died long before we reached our destination.

The sun was going down as Mary wheeled the car through the alley and came to screeching halt outside her back door. I rolled off of the back seat and onto the floor as she slammed the car into park, lending further proof to my earlier stated theory. Well, at least I would've hit the floor if I hadn't become wedged between the front and back seats. I flopped around like a freshly caught trout in a vain effort to free myself from this embarrassing predicament before my lovely caretaker could discover me. No such luck.

"Oh God, are you all right?" came the heroine's voice above the noise of my futile struggles.

Trying to maintain some degree of my cool demeanor, I quietly asked, "Would you mind tilting the front seat forward so I can get out of here?"

Mary did as this supposedly wounded biker asked and I managed to free myself without acting too hurt.

As she helped me through her back door, I asked, "You make a good living as a travel agent, right?"

"Yes, why?"

"I don't think you could make a living as an ambulance driver," I answered as I settled onto her couch, wincing in pain.

Mary was clucking like an old mother hen as she said, "This is the thanks I get for taking you into my home?"

As she settled me on her couch, I just gave her that slow (I think Jackie Collins would call it "smoldering") stare. She fussed over the pillows behind my head before I said, "I told you that I didn't want to put you in any more danger. The people around me don't..." I stopped and touched her arm, drawing her eyes to mine. "I just wouldn't want anything to happen to you after the way you've helped me."

I actually got to see the deep blush come to her features as she said, "What? You mean trying to kill you on the drive over here or almost turning you into the cops?"

I reached out and touched her cheek with my leather-gloved hand and said, "You didn't though, and for that I owe you. And that's not something I'm used to."

Mary struggled to break eye contact with me, helped me take my coat off, and found herself staring at the cold steel weapon that had saved both of our lives (at least, in her eyes). I laid back on the couch and automatically loosened the pistol in its holster. She carried the heavy leather jacket to the hall closet, holding it to her face for a moment just to smell the worn leather. I watched her hang it with her own coats and pull a blanket down from the top shelf. When she returned to the living room, I let my eyes close as I feigned an exhausted sleep. I could feel her studying my features when she paused for a moment too long when she spread her blanket over me. I wondered what she thought of the close-cropped, near white hair and beard, the ice blue eyes hidden from her now. Finally, she decided leave me to my peaceful dreams. As she walked away from me, my left eye opened just a crack and watched her Rocky Mountain Jeans leave the room. I never had written that thank you note.

Chapter 22

When Mary came out of her bedroom the next morning to check on her patient, she found the couch empty. I had left her a handwritten note on the refrigerator door thanking her for the couch space, but that I had to leave. That was all.

I watched her carefully that day, to see what effect, if any, my appearance as Davin Rowan would have on T.G. She spent most of the day in a sort of a trance, not really paying attention to what she was doing. I guess that would explain why a honeymoon couple found themselves de-planing in Nome, Alaska, while a sled-dog team and their driver got to see lovely Hawaii.

I found that I didn't have what it took to watch her from afar for too long at about seven that night when I finally came up with an excuse to go back to her house.

She must have read my mind because she answered the door holding my jacket in her hands. I couldn't tell you what she said for sure in the way of greeting because her perfume was doing its thing to me again, but it was something about would I care to come inside?

"No." I smiled at her slowly. "I just came for this." I reached out and took my coat out of her hands, thanking her for the way she had treated me the night before.

"But, you need a place to stay..." She was looking for a reason, working at it...

"Found a place here in town." I was looking deep into her eyes again. "I'll have to stick around for awhile before I can ride very far."

"How long do you think you'll..." I think Mary was beginning to wonder if she'd ever finish a sentence again.

"Not long. I'd better be going." I stepped back and turned to walk away.

She had to stop me, "Will I see you around town?"

I just smiled at her. "Maybe." And walked away.

"I just can't believe that she hasn't recognized me," I told Andy later on that day when I got back to the little tourist cabin that I'd rented for Davin Rowan's stay in Mel-Ville (get it?).

"We already went over this, Mel." Andy had more confidence in our little plan than I did, obviously. "Your eyes just kind of jump out at her now with that new color, and I doubt that she could've told you what color your eyes were before."

"You mean I look like Rodney Dangerfield now?"

"No, but they are your most striking feature. Your hair and beard definitely call attention away from your features, and that tan makes you look a lot different than you think. I'm telling you, Mel, there's no way anybody could recognize you."

It was about an hour later when I had to go up town to stock the cabin's kitchenette. I wore sunglasses and my attitude just in case I ran into anybody. I really wasn't prepared when I rounded the corner of the drug store and met Susan on the sidewalk. She was reading a paperback as she walked and I quickly ducked my head and tried to slip by her. Sue never even looked up from her heaving bosom literature as she, in passing, said, "Hey, Mel."

She came to a stop when I did and slowly turned to look at me with eyes the size of dinner plates.

"How in the hell did you recognize..."

"When did you join a biker cult?"

I glanced around quickly to see if anyone was watching us before I grabbed Sue by the arm and drug her into an alley.

"I knew it," she was almost shouting, "I knew you were up to something!"

"Would you quiet down." I was looking around for witnesses. "Before somebody decides that I'm robbing you."

We decided that I should come over to her house after dark that night to tell her and Eric what the hell was going on. I walked on with her reminder not to forget still ringing in my ears. Maybe the old Mel would've forgotten, but not now.

I knocked on their back door at about ten, having spent a few minutes ducking a police car that seemed slightly interested in me. Figuring that with my looks and dress, I'd be a natural for a good background check, I didn't want to have to blow what cover I had by explaining myself to one of the local deputies. Eric opened the door and it was suddenly obvious to me that Susan hadn't warned her husband that I was coming. After the door slammed in my face I could hear Eric yelling for Susan to call the police because one of Mary's bikers was outside. I heard Sue's voice next, low and soothing as she explained whom the man outside their back door was.

There was silence for a moment, followed by the door opening just a crack with Eric's left eye peering out at me. After studying me for a few seconds, he whipped open the door and said, "Mel! Good to see you. I thought you weren't gonna be back for another couple of months."

I walked past him into the house and said, "Well, you know how it is, Eric, plans change."

"That isn't the only thing that changes around here." Susan was giving me another one of her looks.

I leaned up against the kitchen counter and crossed my arms over my chest. Letting all of my attitude come to the surface, I asked, "What do ya think, Babe?"

Sue never even blinked as she stuck her finger down her throat and feigned throwing up in the sink.

"That good?" was my answer as I took a seat at the kitchen table where she and Mary had shared that bottle of wine about a hundred years ago.

"Worse than that." Susan was being less than supportive as she and Eric joined me at the table.

Eric's head was bobbing up and down like an ostrich, trying to see anything that looked like the old me as I said, "It's a good thing that I'm not trying to pick you up, then, isn't it?"

"Hey," Eric was suddenly on the defensive, "that's not even funny."

"You see." I waved a hand at Eric as I dropped the Davin personality. "He never had any trouble being jealous before now. It's like I'm different. I'm, I'm..."

"Dangerous." As usual, Sue hit the nail on the head.

"Yeah," I smiled as I said it. "And we know that Mary likes 'em dangerous."

Susan's voice rose to a high-pitched squeal as she said, "You are the mystery biker!"

"What mystery biker?" Eric wanted to know.

I leaned back in my chair and said, "Let me guess, Mary told you, but you didn't tell Eric."

"Didn't tell me what, dear? I've heard the official version, but nothing about any mystery..." There was definite frost in Eric's voice.

"I was going to tell you tonight, honey." She reached out and grabbed Eric's hand on the table. "Mary just told me about it today."

"What was her version of the story?" I asked.

Susan told Eric and I a story that would make Michael Chrichton proud. Not only had Mary embellished the story a little bit, she all but downright lied. According to her perspective, an ice god in leather had burst into her office, saving her from certain death at the hands of two biker executioners. Driving the two seven foot tall killers from her office with a hail of gunfire, this blindingly handsome man had selflessly thrown his own body in front of Mary to save her from two bullets that had been meant for her. Then she had hidden him from the police, feeling as if she had to after he had saved her life. She had taken him to her home to nurse this Adonis back to health, but he had faded away into the night like some kind of storybook hero.

My grin had grown wider and wider throughout this tale, and now my head felt like it was sure to split wide open.

Eric was looking at me with a newborn respect and I stopped grinning long enough to say, "She tells a better story than Steven Speilberg, but don't believe a word of it."

Sue was just staring at the new me with disbelief in her eyes. "I just can't believe that she didn't recognize you."

"What's unbelievable is that you did, I proved that by almost giving Eric a heart attack."

I pointed out to her. "How did you pull that one off?"

She just shook her head and gave me the answer that I expected. "I don't know. It was just you."

"Oh, I see." I snorted at her. "Mary was easy, though. I just never gave her a chance to see who I really was. From the moment I crashed through that door of hers, which I left her money to fix, she saw me as someone that was the complete opposite of Melville. Someone that was dangerous, someone that might break her heart. The kind of man she could fall in love with."

Susan just shook her head and asked, "So are you just going to take advantage of her and leave her in a cloud of tire dust? What exactly is your plan here, Mel? Or do you have one at all?"

I looked at my old friend through strange, ice blue eyes and said, "You know me better than that Sue. I'd never hurt her for anything in the world. Never."

"That's exactly what you're doing, Mel, that's exactly what you're doing."

"I've got a plan," I said after a few moment's silence.

Eric tried to lighten the mood a little. "Then give it to us."

"I just wanted her to notice me. That's all. Now, it's just a matter of time until I tell her who I am."

"Hell of an idea, Mel, I'm sure that will inspire nothing but love and confidence for you in her." Susan sounded as enthusiastic as ever.

I heard the knock at the front door as it swung open. Mary called out, asking if anyone was at home. I frantically sprang towards the back door, but Eric stopped me when it became obvious that trying to leave that way would bring me into Mary's line of sight.

"I'll be right there, Mary," Sue said as she held open the door of her broom closet for Eric to shove me inside.

The door slammed two inches in front of my nose as Mary walked into the kitchen and sat in the chair I'd just left. She slammed her head down on the table and let out a whimper. Now why would that look familiar to me?

Eric and Susan exchanged a look that promised to remind each other to get some normal friends. Sue sat down and slipped an arm around Mary's shoulders and asked gently, "What the hell's the matter now?"

Mary didn't even raise her head as she said, "My life is doomed."

"Well, at least she's being upbeat." Eric had that look going again.

If I stuck my face to the doorjamb and squinted a little bit I could make out Mary at the table. I was trying not to knock anything over and breathe quietly as Mary sat just a few feet away from me, knowing that both an outlaw biker and her best friend were so close.

The Goddess looked up from the table, an endearing little red spot on her forehead where her head hit the table. She took a deep, ragged breath and said, "Why do I always fall in love with the wrong guys?"

"What do you mean, Hon?" I would swear that Susan was staring directly at me.

"I don't know. I just wish that I could meet someone who would treat me like I deserve. Someone that would treat me decent. I just get so tired of falling for guys that don't stay..." Mary wound down quickly. Eric asked her to tell the story again, since he'd only heard Susan's version, so you didn't really know what was true and what wasn't.

T.G. took a deep breath and recounted the story of her fateful meeting with Davin Rowan.

It felt like she'd been sitting behind her desk, staring out the window forever. It had only been about a month since Mel had left on his vacation, but Mary had started missing him the first week. Did she realize that she missed him? That we don't know for sure. What we do know is that she wasn't getting much work done, and she was blaming it on the beautiful mountain spring outside. She felt cooped up, that was it. Maybe she should have went on that trip with Mel. That thought stopped her cold. He had offered to take her along, but he was joking. Wasn't he?

What if he wasn't? What if he really wanted to...Mary shook her head and tried to concentrate on the paperwork in front of her. It didn't work.

They'd met on a kind of date, but he hadn't made anything that was even like a pass at her ever since. He'd treated her like a friend, a good friend. He never made her feel uncomfortable, like she wasn't good enough to be around him. Mary thought about that for a second. He never made her feel like Chris had. Mel made her feel...

The sudden roar of motorcycle engines outside her front door interrupted her thoughts. Mary started to stand up behind her desk when two gunshots rang out and a leather clad body crashed into her front door. Make that through her front door, she thought, as the glass exploded into a million pieces and the blonde-haired man fell in a heap on her lobby carpet. He crawled toward her (or was it toward the safety of her desk), meeting her eyes with his own ice-blue ones as he screamed, "Get down, goddammit, get down!"

Mary stood frozen in fear as she saw two huge men in biker leather suddenly framed in her destroyed doorway. The big tall one aimed his pistol at the prone man on her floor, while the short fat one aimed his pistol at her! Later, Mary would swear that she saw the man on the floor roll over and jerk a pistol from his coat and fire at the two killers in the doorway. But the casual observer (if there had been any) would have told you she couldn't have seen anything from her vantage point under her desk.

Mel's Goddess spent the next few minutes under that desk being very scared.

"Lady?" She heard a man's voice through the ringing silence. "Are you all right?"

Mary slowly peeked over the desk, seeing nothing but the blond man lying in the same spot he had occupied when she dove for the safety of the carpet.

"Who the hell are you?" If you haven't already guessed it, Mary was over being scared and was now well into mad as hell. "And who were those other rabid bikers? Why were they trying to kill you? Why were they trying to kill me?" She paused to take a breath. "Well, are you gonna tell me or are you just going to lay there looking stupid?"

He tried to roll over to stand and fell back to the floor, pain making his face contract. When he tried again, Mary could see two perfect holes in the back of his jacket.

"Oh my god, you've been shot, you should lay still. I should, I should..." She started for the phone on her desk.

"No!" The word came from the wounded man with surprising force. "No cops, lady, they'll be here quick enough anyway."

"What do you mean no cops? We've got to tell them so they can catch those two guys that tried to kill us..." Mary was helping the wounded man try to stand. "Besides that if you don't get to a hospital, you'll die."

He just looked into her eyes with his own sharp, penetrating gaze and said, "No, I won't die." He pulled apart his denim shirt so that she could see the bulletproof vest he wore beneath. "I'll just have to find a place to hole up for a while, I think one of those shots cracked a rib. But thanks for caring anyway."

Mary was starting to feel just a little bit weak in the knees as she said, "You saved my life, didn't you?"

"If I wouldn't have come crashing through your front door in the first place, you would never have been in any danger." His tremendous ice-blue eyes grew downcast as he stated what was obvious to him.

"But if you hadn't driven them off..." Mary was still sure that she had cheated death by a mere fraction of an inch.

Her thoughts were broken by the sound of an approaching siren.

"It's the police, you've got to hide!" She started to pull him towards the back door of her office that led out into the old service bay of this converted gas station. He shook his head even as they entered the garage.

"My bike is out back here, they'll find it for sure." He stopped and looked into her eyes again. "I won't put you in any more danger than I already have."

Mary darted out from under his arm, and robbed of her support so suddenly, he almost fell to the ground. She rushed to the garage door and strained to throw it open. The giant motorcycle was waiting patiently on the other side. The police sirens wailed closer and closer as Mary struggled to push the big hog into the garage. She managed to get it back down on its kickstand without mishap, and slammed the rusty old garage door shut behind her. She tried to run past the biker to get back up to the office before the police came in, but he reached out and grabbed her arm, wincing in pain as he stopped her.

"I can't let you do this..."

Mary just said, "I have to."

After the police had left to place a A.P.B. on the two bikers that shot out Mary's front door and then rode away, Mary went back out into the garage to find "Her Biker" finishing up wrapping his ribs with tape taken from a rather extensive first-aid kit that came from the back of his Harley. She poked through the contents of the afore-mentioned kit to keep from staring at the man's well-muscled, and well-tanned body. Mary found things like suture material, pressure bandages and even a manual on emergency surgery.

"It pays to be prepared in my business." He spoke with a quiet confidence that caused her knees to weaken again.

"What business is that? Window repair?" She always got smart-assed when she was nervous.

He smiled slowly at her joke as he pulled his shirt back on over the tape, groaning as he slid his shoulder holster back into place. "Let's just say I work for some people who listen to a lot of Reggae and wear their hair in corn rows. It's best for you if you don't know too much about me." His eyes grew sad again as he said, "I've got to get out of here though, I'm putting you in too much danger already." Trying to get to his feet, he groaned again and almost fell to the floor.

Again, she slid herself under his arm and helped him to his feet.

"Since you're going to be staying with me for a while, shouldn't you at least tell me your name?" Mary asked as she was walking him to her car.

He resigned himself to her tender care by saying, "It's Davin. Davin Rowan."

"And this Davin just makes things worse, doesn't he?" Susan was being downright cruel as Mary finished her tale.

Eric cleared his throat and I was glad to see that someone was going to stick up for me. "You don't know that for sure, Sue. He could be the perfect man for her."

"No, he can't be." Mary sounded sure. "It wouldn't feel so good if he was going to stick around. Besides, he already told me that he was going to leave as soon as his ribs heal."

"So you just have to stay away from him until he leaves town." Susan being helpful again.

"I just feel like something's missing from my life, like everything's out of focus..." Mary sounded like she couldn't concentrate, and I could sympathize with her on that because her perfume had finally snaked its way into the broom closet and was driving me crazy.

"Yeah." Eric was still on my side. 'Say, have you heard from Mel?"

Mary's eyes didn't even focus as she said, "No. I haven't. I wonder what Davin is doing right now?"

Susan let me out of the closet, literally, after Mary left. The rest of the conversation hadn't been much, just Mary wishing that she hadn't fallen in love with this Davin Rowan. And yes, it was breaking my heart to put T.G. through this, but I didn't have a choice. At least I didn't think I did at this point. Not to mention the fact that putting up with Susan's new guilt trip was driving me crazy.

"When are you gonna tell her?" She was sniping at me before I could even get out the backdoor.

"When I'm ready, Sue. She has to be totally in love with me before I can tell her or it will all be for nothing." I needed to talk to Jake and Andy in the worst way, they were the ones that kept convincing me that I was doing the right thing.

"Listen Mel." It was almost like she'd been reading my mind again. "I know this is really hard on you, it just bothers me that you're doing this to her when I know you don't want to."

"Sue." I put a hand on her shoulder and borrowed a page from Jake's book of tricks. "I am the perfect man for her. No man could treat her better than I can, no man could love her more. If I have to trade a little bit of what I believe in to make her happy for the rest of her life, I'll do it. Okay?"

She wrapped both arms around me and squeezed until my leather squeaked. "All right. I just hope you know what you're doing, for both your sakes."

The ride home that night was longer than it should've been due to a lengthy detour on my part. I rode the big hog up a long mountain road until I could see the lights of my little town far below me. Pulling the motorcycle off the road, I climbed off and sat on a fallen tree, staring out over the lights. It didn't take long for Jake and Andy to find me.

"You know what you want to hear, Mel." Jake was always a psychoanalyst.

"Why don't you tell me anyway."

"We have to do this if she's going to fall in love with you. She has to see you in that way. You heard the way she talked about you tonight. You and Davin. She doesn't even realize that Melville is alive. This will have to work."

"He's right, Mel." Andy had thankfully gotten over her crush on me, and she reached out and rubbed my bent shoulders. She was what I called a "touchy-feely" person, like Mary. "What you told Sue tonight was true, and hopefully she'll see it now. Susan will have to help you if we're going to do this thing. Even with this attitude of yours, we'll need all the help we can get."

I laughed that quiet, thoughtful laugh that held no humor whatsoever as I said, "You guys are pretty long on confidence tonight, aren't you?"

Andy put her lean arm around my shoulders as she said, "We

want you to win, Mel. We want Mary to win. You have to believe that."

"I believe it, Andy," I answered, "I just have a hard time remembering it sometimes."

The three of us sat in silence watching the lights below until the rising sun turned the sky a brilliant red. With all of that thinking under my belt, I decided it was time to go home.

Chapter 23

When I rolled up to the cabin's door, it took a major effort not to react to Mary sitting on my step.

"Remember, cracked ribs and danger all around you," Andy whispered in my ear as I stepped of the Harley.

"Hi," Mary said as she jumped up and brushed the dirt off. It was not lost on me that she was wearing a really nice outfit. Not the regular work clothes, definitely date material.

"How did you find me?" It came out kind of harsh as I grabbed her arm, glancing around like a CIA agent looking for snipers in the surrounding forest, and towed her into the cabin, slamming the door shut behind her.

I made sure to wince as I took off my jacket and slung it over a chair. Mary sat down in the same chair and grabbed the jacket, holding it as casually as she could. For some reason, she really loves that jacket. I decided to find out why.

"What's with you and that jacket?" I asked in a sharp tone, telling myself over and over that I was Davin Rowan, not some mushy writer.

Mary just looked down and buried her nose in the leather, too embarrassed to say anything.

"Well?" I was really beginning to hate this guy.

She looked at me with sudden shock and pain in her eyes, not used to such insensitive questions. At first, I didn't think she was going to answer me at all, but soon enough she started to talk.

"My father was a State Patrolman for thirty-two years." Suddenly, the thing with Chris made a lot more sense than it ever had. "And I can remember when he would come home, morning or night, I would run to him. He would swing me into the air and hold me tight against his chest until I squealed for him to stop. I loved him so much and I knew that he loved me too. He's the only man that stayed in my life until the day he died. He was always there for me whenever I needed him." She stopped to wipe at the tears in her eyes. "But he always smelled the same, gun oil and leather. Just like this jacket, gun oil and leather."

"How did he die?" It was amazing to me that we had never talked about this in all of our conversations over coffee. It also scared me a little.

"He had a heart attack when I was twelve. My mom never remarried, I don't think she ever even dated anyone."

"I'm sorry to hear that," was what came out of my mouth, but it wasn't what was going on in my head. I wanted to tell her that I loved her, that I would never leave her, that I was the man she'd been looking for. All this and more I wanted to tell her, but Jake and Andy were holding me firmly in check. "Let her open up to you," Jake was whispering, "let her tell you everything she wants to, the more she says, the better chance we have of giving her what she needs."

"It's not fair..." I said to Jake through clenched teeth.

"What?" Mary was drying her eyes as she looked up at me.

"I was just thinking..." C.Y.A. is what I was thinking, "that it's not fair that you've been treated so badly."

"My father treated me better than..." Mary was mad as hell that I would say something like that.

"Not your father, Mary. All the other men in your life."

Now she looked suspicious. "What could you know about the men in my life?"

"Well." I sat on the arm of her chair. "I'm guessing they don't stay like they should. They don't treat you as well as you deserve to be treated. Any man in his right mind would know that you should be treated like a queen." I slowly reached out and touched her cheek with the back of my hand, smiling down at her. "And would make any sacrifice to spend the rest of his life with you."

Her eyes were unfocused again as I stood up and walked away from her. I'd swear that I heard her quietly say, "Wow."

"Let's go for a ride."

Now the obvious problem with this is that I'm supposed to be hiding out and all of the sudden I want to go for a motorcycle ride. The truth of the matter is that I couldn't stay in that cabin for another second and still trust myself with the highly vulnerable Ms. Byrd. Mary didn't seem to notice the contradiction in my plan of action, though, so I decided to split the difference and take her up the mountain.

You never could have told me how good it feels to ride down a twisting mountain road with the arms of someone you care about more than anything else in the world wrapped tightly around your waist. I never would have believed you that it could be that good. It can.

I pulled up and shut the bike off on the banks of a clear mountain lake that I'd discovered on one of my morning runs. It was almost five miles from town, and the temperature of the water was downright chilly from the snowmelt even as late as May, so we had the entire lake to ourselves.

Mary shed my coat as she stepped off of the bike and draped it over the seat. She grabbed my hand and led me to an outcropping of granite that overlooked the scenic view before us. We sat down and listened to the waves lap the shore for a minute or two before she asked, "When are you leaving?"

"I'm going to have to stay another month for my ribs to heal, but I have to leave soon after that if I'm ever going to go."

Mary was looking at me, studying me almost, trying to figure out what I meant. I turned and did that smiling into her eyes thing that Judith Krantz loves so much, and got to watch as the light came to her eyes. It was quickly followed by one of the cutest blushes I'd ever seen as she ducked her head to avoid my gaze.

We spent the rest of the morning sitting on that rock and talking about whatever came to mind. What kept coming to my mind was that here I sat, with a woman that I tell myself I care about, lying to her about who I was. She was telling Davin about things that she never even came close to telling Mel, being open and honest to me, and I couldn't tell her the truth.

I was feeling very low as I drove back into town, still very conscious of her arms around me. I stopped at her office to let her off.

"Come to lunch with me," she said, "I want you to meet a friend of mine."

There was no getting out of it. Believe me, I tried. Here I was, sitting at "our" table waiting for Sue to join us, trying to hide behind a pair of Gargoyles and hanging my head in case anybody else might be able to recognize me. Mary was snuggled up against me in the booth, still wearing my jacket. It was not completely lost on me that I had become just like her last boyfriend to get to this point, but I was taking some small comfort in the fact that I was not going to be this way for the rest of my life. Knowing that helped a little bit, but not enough to make me forget that I had turned on what I believed in most in life, and I wasn't sure that I could ever get it back.

Was she worth it? I turned and looked into her eyes as she smiled up at the man who wasn't me. I can't describe the way she made me feel, but I knew that whatever it took it would be more than worth it.

I was hoping that Sue was as good an actor as I was when I heard the door open and she came in. While she was walking over to us it was impossible for me to read her face at all, and that was making me more nervous than anything else. Usually, I can tell what Sue is thinking just by looking at her, but now, she was blank.

"Hiya, Sue!" Mary said. I wanted to drag myself outside and throw myself in front of a truck when I figured out where I'd heard that tone in Mary's voice before. It was just how she'd sounded when she sat down at our table with Chris Lucas. You remember, the Gray Brother incident.

Of course, now I could see what Sue was thinking. She wanted to throw me under that same truck I was thinking about. Sitting down across from us, she said a polite hello to me as Mary introduced Davin Rowan.

"So, Davin is it?" Sue asked with a tight smile. "What do you do?"

I'd never got around to giving Sue the run down on Rowan's past, so I really played up my part. "Let's just say," I paused for disgustingly obvious dramatic effect and scanned the restaurant to see if anyone was eavesdropping, "that I'm a private contractor for a Caribbean conglomerate of businessmen." I slowly glanced over at Mary to find that she was finally giving me the prized "gaga" look, it was just too bad that it was Davin she was looking at.

"Does that mean," Sue wasn't going to let me off that easy, "that you're a bartender in one of those cheap little places that uses two thousand cocktail umbrellas a day? Or are you a banana boat captain?"

I leaned forward and gave her one of my best growls. "You don't want to go there, pet lady."

Susan almost bought my tough guy act. I could tell by the way that she had to stifle a belly laugh. I looked at Mary (slowly again) and said something about how it didn't look like her friend believed me.

Sliding out of the booth I told Mary that I would find her later and walked out the door. Outside, I could see Mary and Susan through the front window, and it looked like Mary was really giving Susan hell. I threw one leg over the bike as Mary left the booth in a huff. Susan looked through the window at me and I gave her one of those "cocky fighter pilot" grins and a double thumbs up.

Mary came running out of the diner and grabbed my arm as I started the bike.

"Don't go, Davin, please."

I just turned to her and held out my hand to help her onto the bike. It's amazing to me that if you keep your mouth shut, people can only think that you're an idiot, but if you say too much you can prove it to them. She got on.

I could see Sue's mouth moving as we drove away. I'm sure it wasn't kind words.

"She just doesn't understand," Mary said as I helped her off the bike back at the travel agency's back door.

"Understand what?" I was still pulling that "just keep your mouth shut" thing. It works, really.

"She just doesn't understand the way I feel about you. She told me that she doesn't want me to get hurt again." She was giving me that look again.

"I don't want that either. But I can't promise you it won't happen," I said as I started the bike and drove away. It was a good thing that I couldn't see her standing in that alley watching me go, or I would've turned that hog around and told her everything.

"I'm weak, I admit it. We've got to tell her."

"We can't." Andy's answer was no real surprise. "You're nearly home free, Mel. She's almost over the edge, but not yet."

"She's right, Mel, you can't tell her yet, but soon." Jake was sticking up for Andy for a change, which surprised me.

"When did you join her side, Jake? You two have been at each other's throat since she's been around."

"Maybe we decided that it was time to call a truce," he answered.

"You just don't want me to go off the deep end before this is over, do you?" It was my turn to see the world from Jake's eyes.

"Yeah, that's pretty much it." At least he was honest.

198

Chapter 24

Things were really bad now. I know, I know, I've got what I wanted most in life and now I'm not happy. It was starting to look like I'd gripe if they delivered the wrong color of free Ferrari. Lying to Mary was really taking its toll on me more than my new personality ever would, and that was mostly because it was something I didn't have much experience with. Actually, I had no idea what I was doing here; lying to a woman was never something I had a real firm grasp of. All right, all right, I'd tried it before, but Mom knew what really happened to that sweater Grandma had knitted for me. It was kind of like that magician's trick with the colored hankies the way she just kept pulling yarn out of the garbage disposal. Not a good scene.

I guess the point is that I'm no good at lying to people, and now it was more important than ever that I do just that. Mary was falling head over heels for this scum bucket Davin Rowan, and it was just what I wanted, I think. The way I was accomplishing this was also enough to make my skin crawl. In the last month's time I had stood up that lovely little travel agent at least four times a week and still managed to spend enough time with her to be sure and tell her many times over that I wouldn't be around much longer.

My imagination could have been running away with me, but it was starting to feel to me like she was reacting differently to my thinly veiled threats of imminent departure. She almost pushed me away when I mentioned it, instead of clinging to me like a little girl as she did at the first. I wasn't really sure what it meant, but I was hopeful that it was good for her.

The last day of the month that I had given myself to tell her came much sooner than I thought it would, or wanted it to. The whole thing couldn't last much longer anyway, my poor conscious just wouldn't take much more of this. At least that's what I was telling myself when I opened my cabin door to find Mary dressed in a bathing suit and cut-off shorts with a man's swim suit in her left hand and a bottle of suntan oil in the other. Oh my God.

"Let's go for a swim."

I just nodded and grabbed a couple of towels out of the bathroom as I changed into the suit, pulling my jeans on over the top, knowing if I tried to talk to her right then that I would be right back to the terminal case of brain fade that started this whole thing more than a year ago. To say that she looked great could be the biggest understatement since the captain of the Hindenburg said, "Do I smell smoke?"

As we cruised through the town on the Harley, I noticed the people turning to look at her as we went by. Funny thing, though, it didn't really make me jealous. Well, okay, maybe a little bit, but mainly it made me feel kinda good. Not that she was with me or anything, I'm not that big a chauvinist, but that they were looking at her because she was beautiful.

I also caught one or two ladies checking out yours truly. That does wonders for your self-confidence, let me tell you.

When we pulled up at the lake, I found us a stretch of beach that was deserted and was simply enjoying the mountain view when Mary took off her shorts and caused a major sensory overload. I was trying to look everywhere but at her until she called out for me to join her. I figured it was safe to look because I could hear her splashing around in the water but I was wrong. Swallowing my heart and several other body parts that weren't where they were supposed to be, I managed to look Mary directly in the eyes, not letting my eyes drop the whole time I was stripping down to the shorts she'd brought me. The truth was that if I looked anywhere else I was likely to embarrass myself.

I splashed into the chilled water and she took my hand in hers and headed for the deep, clear water. When I couldn't see anything but her head above the water, I relaxed. A lot. Have you ever heard that men are very visual creatures? That is no lie. As I relaxed, in spite of myself I started to have fun. In no time, I was laughing with her as she splashed water at me and I splashed back. We swam for a long time, playing the games that people have been playing since...well, forever.

We played until she swam in close and made a grab at my swimsuit. It wasn't like she was making a serious pass at me or anything, just a playful grab. It was enough to make me think for a second. I headed for the shore, ashamed of myself for what I'd been doing. Grabbing a towel, I sank down to the blanket that I'd spread before, when I was looking at anything but Mary. I dried off a little bit, but just didn't have the heart to do too much as T.G. came up and sat down beside me. I really couldn't look at her now, I was hating myself more than ever.

Her hands were folding and unfolding again as she asked, "Don't you like being around me? Is that it?"

Finally, I let the words come out. "You're perfect, Mary, no man could ever ask for more in a friend or a lover than you."

"Then is it that I'm not beautiful enough for you?"

"Please don't cry, Mary, please. You're the most beautiful woman in the entire world."

She just looked at me for a second, wanting more. I'd been waiting for this a long time, so I had more to give.

"Do you remember Helen of Troy, Eve of the Garden, Cleopatra?"

"Yes..." she said.

"Dogs. All of them real woofers."

So much for worrying about her crying. Mary laughed as I grinned back at her until she remembered what this discussion was about.

"What is it then?"

I thought about it for a long time before I automatically picked up a towel and turned her until her back was to me and started to dry her hair. I talked while I rubbed at her dark locks.

"It's just that I don't want to..." I stumbled over the words, feeling more like my old self than I have in months. "I can't let myself hurt you, and that's where this whole thing is headed."

"I know you can't stay forever." She turned around to face me and was suddenly very, very close. This time, I really could feel her body heat, it wasn't just my imagination. "But I'm a big girl. I want this for us, even if you leave tonight, it will be worth it."

The ride back to my cabin was a lot shorter than I remember it being, her arms around me feeling different somehow. I felt strange, at once more secure than I had felt in a long time, and still hating myself for what I was about to do. She was near me now, and she did want to touch me, everything I'd ever dreamed of had come true, for someone else. For Davin Rowan.

Mary was holding onto me very tight as we walked through the door of the cabin and she let go of my hand to let my faithful leather jacket slide to the floor. I lost track of everything but her as she came into my arms and touched her lips to mine. Mary became all there was in my world as her touch brought feelings in me to the surface that I had buried too long.

Then I felt it. Something was wrong. I knew what my problem was, but this was something wrong with her. The feeling built until our kiss broke and we both blurted out, "I can't do this!"

We just stared at each other for a moment until I said with a style that was more Melville than Davin, "Tell me."

"I'm in love with someone else."

Oh God, not another boyfriend to watch and wait my way through, I couldn't take that.

She didn't stop. "I don't think I ever realized that I loved him until this moment, but there is something in you that reminds me of him and I think that's what attracted me to you in the first place."

Had I figured her wrong? Wasn't she attracted to the rebel love 'em and leave 'em type? What kind of man would I have to become for her to love me? I hung my head low, thinking about "you're so great but you're just not the right guy for me" as I asked, "Who is this guy?"

She jumped off the bed and pulled on her cut-offs (when the hell had that happened?) as she said, "He's a writer."

What?

What was that?

"She said he's a writer, Mel," Jake and Andy were both screaming at me. "She's talking about you!"

Maybe she knows another writer?

"I've been in love with him for a long time, and just didn't know it." She said as she opened the door.

"Where are you going?" I asked.

She stopped in mid-stride and came back to the bed, where I had yet to move a muscle, leaned in, kissed my cheek and said, "France."

The door slammed behind her and I found myself staring at my leather jacket lying on the floor. I came out of it when Andy actually slapped me.

"You've got to get to Paris!"

I don't remember much after that for awhile.

The front tire on the Harley locked up and it almost dumped me off on the sidewalk as I came to a screeching halt outside of the local hair salon. I jumped off the bike and ran through the front door, scaring the hell out of the little old lady sitting under the hair dryer. Whipping off my jacket, I sat down in the empty chair.

"Give me a shave and dye my hair dark brown." I told the woman in the floral print smock that was just standing there giving me one of those funny looks, who also happened to be Eric's sister. There is a real bad blind date story here, but I'll save that for another time.

"We don't give shaves, but I can wax your facial hair if you want."

Ouch. "There's a twenty in it for you if you use a razor."

"I can work with that." She said as she went to work putting me back to the way I was supposed to be.

As she returned my chair to the up-right position and draped a towel over my head to dry my now normal hair, I reached underneath the towel, removed the ice blue contacts and threw them at the wastebasket. When she whipped the towel off of me, I grinned into the mirror and said, "Hiya, Sandy, how ya been?"

She just looked at me in shock for a while before she said, "Melville, where the hell did you come from?"

"I'd love to tell you, Sandy, but I'm kind of in a hurry." I put a twenty on the counter as I bolted out the door, and almost killed myself trying to put on my jacket and start the bike at the same time.

I needed help if I was gonna pull this off.

Parking the bike behind the pet store, I rounded the corner headed for the front door on the run. I happened to look through the window and saw Susan facing the window talking to...

Mary! I tried to slide to a stop but my feet flew out from under me and I found myself lying on the sidewalk staring at the sky. Ouch again. Crawling back around to the alley didn't look real good, but it kept Mary from spotting me as she left the pet store and drove off down the street.

I came around the corner again to find Susan on the sidewalk checking for bloodstains.

"Did you tell her?" The whole thing was blown wide open if Susan had told Mary what she knew.

"I don't know why, but I didn't tell her anything."

I almost did another flip right there before I said, "I need your help..."

"Mel!" Susan yelled to stop me as I bolted out the door a few minutes later, herself on the way to slow Mary down as much as she could.

I turned to look back at her as she said, "It's good to have you back."

"It's good to be back, Sue. See you soon."

Chapter 25

It didn't take me long to pack a few things for the trip. What took forever was getting a flight schedule figured out that wouldn't have me crossing paths with a certain travel agent headed in the same direction. By the time I finished juggling things around, I was headed to Paris via Alaska, Australia, Siberia and Morocco. There's a reason I'm not a travel agent.

From what Susan had told me, I had the arrival times as close as I could get them. The hard part was going to be getting to the hotel ahead of Mary, but I'd worry about that as the time came.

I hit the (Montana) airport two hours ahead of Mary's flight time, which she would more than make up in the air. I still had to run behind a baggage cart to get by the lounge where she sat reading a magazine. Pausing for a second once I was past to watch her, she threw down the magazine and looked at her watch in frustration. I would have swore that she said my name, as she looked at the departure times and doubtless saw the back of one rapidly receding traveler.

"Why?" I wanted to know. "Why can't I tell her here?"

Andy paced beside me as we headed for the gate. "You are fulfilling one of her fantasies, Mel. You remember what she said about Paris in the spring."

"But isn't it pretty much summer now?" I had to ask.

Andy just gave me a hopeless look and said, "We're using romantic license here, Mel, and so will Mary, believe me. And besides that, what could be more romantic than a rendezvous in Paris? Really, Mel, you got to start thinking of these things yourself if you want to keep Mary happy."

I was sitting on the plane before that statement really hit me full force. Mary was coming to Paris to find me and tell me that she loved me.

"It's great, isn't it?" Jake was sitting beside me on the nearly deserted DC-10 as it wheezed its way towards Alaska. A sudden cough in the engines and a sudden loss of altitude made me wish I'd tried to get on Mary's flight and just spent the whole time hiding from her in the bathroom.

"She's coming for you, Mel." Andy was on the other side now. "How do you feel?"

"Uh huh," was all I could manage to spit out, before I leapt out of my seat to rush for the tiny bathroom at the back of the plane.

Jake looked over at Andy and said, "I hope he gets over this before we get there."

Barely. By the time we hit the ground in Paris I was ready to face the woman I loved, especially now that she loved me too. I breezed through customs with nothing more than a couple of shirts, a pair of jeans, and my leather jacket, and found myself looking for a cab with what I needed. A glance at the arrival boards in the terminal behind me showed me that Mary's plane was landing while I stood there.

"I get you there quick," a cabby said as he leaned out of the window of his Saab. I gave a quick glance at the cab, and saw the marks of some serious high-speed collisions. This was my kind of guy.

"You've got it, buddy," I said as I threw my bag into the back seat. "And enough extra to buy your lady a beautiful present if we get there alive."

I'd swear we hit warp seven before the next intersection. The traffic whizzed by us at an incredible rate as Pierre (no kidding) turned around in his seat to introduce himself, making me only a little jumpy.

"Look out!" I yelled as he whipped the little car across three lanes of traffic to zip down a side street. I wasn't really worried about us, I just wanted to give the pedestrians a fighting chance. I guess it's just my American sense of fair play.

With a screech of tires that would have made Al Unser proud, my cabby made a perfect parallel parking exhibition in a space that shouldn't have been big enough for a bicycle. I leapt (well, pried myself) out of the cab and gave my new best friend enough money to feed his family for a week. (Or wash his car, I've never been any good at exchange rates. I usually have trouble getting the right change out of a Coke machine).

Finding myself in front of the extremely stylish (and expensive) Hotel DeVille on the Rue De Rivoli, I realized just how good a travel agent Mary really was. I was running for the counter at break-neck speed, with no idea how far Mary was behind me. Trying to tell the concierge (of course, here they call him "that guy behind the counter") who I was, and getting to my room turned out to be easier than I thought it would be as they seemed to be expecting me due to a call from a very lovely lady by the name of Sue. I'd have to remember to ask her how many years of high school French she had taken in preparation for saving my life. I was immediately "assigned" a bellhop that was given orders to help me in any way possible as a woman was coming very soon to meet me and everything must be perfect. I realized that, apparently, Sue could at least say "big tipper" in French as I walked through the door of the suite that had been prepared for me. After the crummy little motel room in the city, this place was paradise.

I quickly took a shower and changed into fresh clothes. Locating my bellboy was easy, he was sleeping in a chair outside my room.

"Hey, Jake." I shook his shoulder and he stood to all of his five feet, and tried to correct me.

"Jacques," he said, tapping his chest with his thumb as he repeated his name. At least I think that's what he said, but to me it sounded like...

"That's what I said, Jake. Where would be a good romantic place to meet a lady?" I was hoping that he at least understood English, but mimed playing the violin and described an hourglass shape in the air in front of me.

I was hoping he wouldn't send me to a female violinist when he pointed downstairs and said, "Café on sidewalk."

"Gotcha, buddy, thanks!" I was off to the races again, scooting down the stairs at about nine-o. I rounded the corner (I really should stop doing that) and almost went head over heels again as I saw Mary talking to the guy behind the counter. Her back was to me so I managed to catch his eye and wave toward the street café. I realized that this was going to cost me some serious coin as he winked broadly at me and pointed T.G. towards the sidewalk.

I sprinted up the stairs, thinking that if I knew Mary as well as I thought I did, I had about a minute while she stopped at a mirror for just a second to make herself presentable. I knew she wasn't going to take the time to take a shower before looking for me, and that made me feel, well, kind of special.

Almost running Jake down, I blurted out, "How can I get down there from up here."

He just shrugged and said, "Window?"

As I climbed down a conveniently located rose trellis (God does love romance), I realized that you usually climb up these things to a romantic interlude, not down. I jumped into a chair and attempted to look relaxed as Jake brought me a drink (how the hell had he gotten down here so fast?) and saw by the way his eyes were moving that Mary was coming up behind me.

"You're Melville." It was Andy and Jake at the same time.

"I'm who I always was," I answered, as calm as I've ever been.

Her touch on my shoulder made me turn. I never would have guessed how good it would feel to look on her with my own eyes. I stood to face her and found that I couldn't say anything. Mary just looked at me and didn't say anything either for a few moments.

Finally, she said, "I decided to take you up on your offer."

"Mary," I finally managed to say without Jake jump-starting my lingual abilities, "God, am I glad to see you."

I wrapped my arms around Mary and held her gently as she said, "We've got to talk."

Holding one of the wrought iron chairs away from the table for her, I noticed that she was shaking in the chill of the spring sunset. Feeling like some kind of lord, I beckoned for the ever present Jake the bellboy to come over and asked him to bring my jacket from my room. Watching his rapidly shrinking back, I realized that I was going to be putting his kids through college.

Taking my seat again, I let Mary reach across the table and take my hand. The pleasured surprise in my eyes was real, as I played my sensitivity card one more time.

"Tell me."

"After you left, I met someone."

She was waiting for me to do my stunted jealousy thing, but I never believed in burning my bridges before I crossed them. So I just said, "Go on."

"I almost fell in love with him, he was gorgeous with just that little bit of danger that you know I love. But at the last second, I realized that the things that attracted me to him, were the things I've always loved in you. Always will love in you."

"You may want to take that back..." I said as I heard Jake approaching from behind us. He handed me my leather jacket and I stood to drape it over Mary's shoulders, settling in my chair as quick as I could, so I could see her reaction. It wasn't what I expected. She just wrapped the coat around her tightly and buried her nose in the leather, breathing in the scent of it.

"My memories aren't the only reason I love this coat. I love this old thing because it belongs to you Mel."

"You knew..."

Mary nodded her head and said, "I figured it out on the way over here. The way you dried my hair at the beach, the way you held me, and how you always listened to me, no matter what." See, I told you it worked, even if I didn't believe it myself.

"And besides," Mary went on, "when I said that it was the things in you that attracted me to him, I meant it. The more time I spent with Davin, the more he reminded me of you."

I thought about that for a second before I said, "I think that was because the more I was around you, the less I could act like some tough guy hitman. I had to be myself, no choice."

She just smiled and said, "I guess you're the first man who ever turned into a nice guy because of hanging around me, and the only reason you did was because that was who you were all along."

I watched Mary struggle for a moment before she said, "You've been helping me all along, haven't you?"

"What do you mean?" I asked, shocked that I could manage to help anyone.

"The way I look for relationships that won't work or where I'll get hurt. I don't need to do that any more. I think it's because of the way you treat me, the way you help me."

My mind wandered back to my research on relationships before I said, "If you've made a change in your life, I can't take any credit for that. That was something that you would've had to do on your own, for yourself. I couldn't help you, no matter how much I wanted to. You've come a long way since I've known you, in a good direction."

Mary smiled as she said, "So have you, Mel, so have you."

What followed was a silence that was uncomfortable for me because I could easily imagine the anger building up in T.G. over what I'd done to her. I was sure that she was going to blow up at any minute as I said, "Aren't you going to kill me now?"

She just shook her head as she said, "I really wanted to. When it first came to me who Davin Rowan really was, I wanted nothing more than to squeeze your neck until your head exploded. I just couldn't believe that you would ever lie to me like that. But, luckily, it was a long flight and I had time to realize that you did all that to make me see you in a romantic way, and how can I hate any man who loves me so much that he puts himself through everything you did?"

She did that smiling into my eyes thing as we sat in that little sidewalk café, and all I could do was smile back.

Did I ever mention that I love this woman?

It was more than two weeks later when I sat down at my word processor again, the house changing around me as I watched in amazement. Mary was just a blur of activity as she set about making the place habitable. The two weeks I'd just spent were without a doubt the best of my life. We had spent them exploring Paris together, finding all of the little out of the way cafés and shops, not to mention finding out a lot about each other. We discovered what Jake had always known, that we were perfect together.

I was just sitting and staring at my battered IBM word processor, wondering what the Axeman would come up with next, when I realized that Jake and Andy had been absent from my life since the moment that Mary had joined me in Paris. I missed them.

"Don't make me cry." It was Jake.

"I wasn't sure if you were ever going to come back." I hoped I sounded as worried as I was.

"We'll always be there if you really need us, Mel," Andy said as she joined us and for the first time since I'd known them, the M.P.H.'s looked, well, sad.

"That sounds like a good-bye, Andy." I was struggling hard now. Jake had been with me for so long, I couldn't imagine what life would be like without him, and Andy had grown to be very close to me. "You've changed a lot in the last few months, Jake, you're actually not too bad to be around now." I smiled to pull some of the bite out of my words. "And you, Andy, you helped get me where I wanted to be."

"The change in me came because of the changes happening in you, Mel. Now it's time that you started writing the things that you're really capable of. No more of this "smoking gun adventure" stuff. It's time you joined the bunch you belong in. Keats, Shelly, Thoreau, Kerouac..." Jake said.

"Who?" I asked.

"That's what I thought," Jake answered. "But there's still the likes of Stoker, Dickens, and that guy that wrote the one about the white whale."

We stared at each other for a second before Andy finished, "As far as your book on women goes, all I did was help you to find the truth in a sea of re-hashed information, Mel. These others that Jake talked about, you have it in you to go as far as they did, maybe further. All you have to do is try."

With that, they were gone. Leaving my life in much the same manner as they entered it, without so much as a "by your leave." It was a part of them that I really liked, and now, it's a part of me.

The phone rang as I sat there thinking about the future and where it might take us, and I reached for the brand new extension right beside my processor.

"Mel? This is Rick Jamison..."

I lost track of what he was saying due to the very lovely travel agent that chose this moment to take a seat in my lap and start chewing on my left ear.

"What...what was that, Rick?"

"I thought we decided that you were going to write a book about how to pick up women and you send me a blank disk?" He really sounded mad. I really didn't care.

"That disk isn't blank, Rick." I wondered if he could hear my lips on Mary's neck.

"It might as well be. 'Just be yourself and don't give up.' One sentence Mel? What the hell is that supposed to..."

It was hard for me to hear any more as the receiver slipped from my hand to the floor. I had better things to occupy my time with than crusty editors.

Mary laughed when her lips were able, and held up her left hand to the Montana sunlight slanting in through the window. The diamond on her ring finger shone as she said, "It's beautiful, Mel."

"Not as beautiful as you."

The fuzzy rat climbed the difficult northern face of my arm to jump across to Mary's shoulder. I watched as he buried his nose in the hair covering her ear, and heard him make a noise of some kind.

Mary's eyes were wide as I asked, "What did he say?"

"He said," she didn't look like she was believing her own ears, "Herman."

I started to laugh out loud and Mary joined me. I squeezed her until she squealed for me not to stop, and it wasn't long before we were concentrating on the more serious matters at hand.

You know what? Life is good.